THE TREEKEEPERS

THE TREEKEEPERS

SUSAN McGEE BRITTON

DUTTON CHILDREN'S BOOKS

NEW YORK

Library of Congress Cataloging-in-Publication Data

Britton, Susan.
 Treekeepers / by Susan McGee Britton.—1st ed.
  p. cm.
Summary: Searching for her father, Bird joins three other children, Issie, Dren, and Stoke, on a journey to the Kingdom of Wen to overthrow the evil Lord Rendarren.
 ISBN 0-525-46944-3
 [1. Fantasy. 2. Fathers and daughters—Fiction.] I. Title.
PZ7.B78075 Tr 2003
[Fic]—dc21   2002040801

Published in the United States by Dutton Children's Books,
a division of Penguin Young Readers Group
345 Hudson Street, New York, New York 10014
www.penguinputnam.com

DESIGNED BY TIM HALL • PRINTED IN USA
First Edition
1 3 5 7 9 10 8 6 4 2

FOR DOUG, WHO KNEW AND CHOSE AND LOVED THIS STORY FIRST

For help in all kinds of weather, I would like to thank my sons and their wives (Zach, Holly, Josh, Paige, Luke, and Betsy Britton), Laura McGee Kvasnosky, Carmen Andres, Sands Hall and her Gold River Gang, and Lucia Monfried.

CONTENTS

THE TREEKEEPERS

1

THE GLIMMERING VIAL

Who can sing of the thalasse, the Holder's burning touch?
Its truth is more than song can tell,
For it bears the light of stars,
The sword stars of the north,
And the lovers' soft candles of the south.
It makes our stone hearts to be ashamed and turn and love,
It causes us to laugh and weep and wonder,
It rescues us from death and tears and stumbling,
It calls us to surrender to the Holder,
As waves surrender to the sea-soaked cliffs.

—*FOREST SONGS,* BY LONGSTILL, WATCHMAN OF WEN

THE young child Piper lay shivering on the heap of dirty straw that was her bed. Her breath came in rattling gasps. The orphan Bird laid her hand upon Piper's forehead. It felt clammy as a frog. Bird had already gathered every bit of clothing, rag, or straw she could find—anything to pile on Piper to make her warm again—to no avail. Despite the summer's heat, despite the straw and rags, Piper shook with cold. Now Bird pulled from her tunic pocket a tattered cloth somewhat larger than a human face and smoothed it over the sick child. In the dusky light, the cloth glinted like the robe of a king, for it was embroidered all over with gold.

It was evening, in deep summer, in a stone room high in an abandoned lordhouse. Bird sat back on her heels and considered what to do next. She was eleven or twelve years old, she didn't know for sure which, and small for her age. Her thin white face often, as now, wore a concentrated frown. Sometimes Bird wished she were Piper's mother. But Piper's real mother was Twist, the beggar girl. Twist was sleeping now, in the corner of the room, her face wet from crying as she slept.

Piper's blue eyes flew open and fixed on Bird. "Bid," she said, and fought for another breath. Piper was only two. She couldn't say Bird's name right yet. Bird saw in Piper's eyes an expectation of comfort and help, neither of which she thought she could give, but she would try. She lifted Piper—rags, straw, tattered cloth and all—and rocked her. The tiny girl didn't even whimper; she just kept trying to breathe. Only the day before, Piper had been healthy, and Bird had fixed her soft brown hair into a tuft on top of her head, tied with blue yarn to match her eyes. The tuft was still there, a small flower of hair, and it brushed Bird's cheek.

Piper had cat's fever. She was going to die. Folk with cat's fever always did.

Twist sat straight up and shook herself. "How is she?" she asked, reaching her thin arms for her child.

"The same," Bird said, still rocking Piper, reluctant to give her up. This might be the last time she would ever hold her.

In the street below, a mother called her children home. Bird touched the woolly loops of Piper's hair bow. The yarn had been a gift from Farwender, who sold sweaters in the market. More of Farwender's yarn, red and yellow, decorated Bird's own hair, which she had tied in four ponytails, one on the top, one on the back, and one on each side of her head. Farwender! His name zoomed through Bird's mind like a shooting star. Maybe he could help! She yielded Piper to Twist's arms and jumped up. "I've got to go," she said, and ran from the room, down the curling stone stairs of the lordhouse.

It was a scary thought, fetching Farwender. He lived far off in the barren hills, where folk in their right minds never went. She had never been there before, even during the day. She didn't tell Twist her plans. Twist had enough worries.

Some wildling boys were wrestling in the ruins of the great hall. As she sped by, one shouted out, "Is that stupid baby dead yet?"

"Shut your mouth, wormlips," she hollered back and rushed out the door, into the gathering night, into the ruined town of Graynok.

Graynok had once been a lovely town, famous for rock courtyards, splashing fountains, and sweet figs. But a few years ago, it had been ravaged by the cruel Lord Rendarren, who was almost finished conquering the whole world. All the rich and strong folk had fled, leaving behind only grayhairs and lamelegs, wildlings and fools, to live out their years in Graynok's moldering remains.

Bird trotted a shortcut through zigzag stone streets, past rubble piles, a cracked dry fountain, and a noseless statue of a warrior. Soon she passed through the gap in the wall where the town gates had once held fast. As night fell, she set her bare feet on the dusty road that led to Farwender's, and everywhere else.

A wide-grin moon that kept sliding behind clouds lit her way. The swelling dry-grass hills looked like giant monsters sleeping under rugs. She set a double-quick marching pace, as she had seen the soldiers use when they came to destroy Graynok.

She had met Farwender in the market, where he sold hats, socks, and sweaters he knit from the wool of his own sheep. He came twice a week, Sword Day and Flower Day. He was always glad to see her. She swept his stall and arranged his wares for sale. He paid her with thick slabs of bread, dripping with thistle honey made by his bees.

Everyone in Graynok—except Bird—thought Farwender's hats and sweaters were ugly. He used wild colors and gaudy patterns of flowers, checks, and stars. Although Farwender loved everything he knit and was always giving his work fond pats, he was only able to sell anything because of his cheap prices.

One, two, one, two, Bird's bare feet poufed the deep road dust, still warm from baking in the sun. The air smelled of dry straw, and crickets rasped. She squared her back and sang to keep her spirits up, a soldiers' marching song. "Hularp, hularp, our arms are strong, our swords are sharp; hayled, hayled, we slice, we thrust, till blood is shed."

Although Bird couldn't get Farwender to talk about it, she was sure he had once been a soldier. He had knife scars on the backs of his hands. And when he stripped down to his half tunic to unload things in the summer heat, you could see a long thick scar on his left side, as if someone had cut him deeply there with a sword.

Farwender was always telling folk that he lived where the road crossed Rilla Nilla River, and that he kept a lantern lit above his door "so those in need will know where to knock." The wildlings made fun of him. "How's he going to help?" they would taunt. "Give them one of his funny hats to wear?" The wildlings would try to steal Farwender's money when he seemed to be counting stitches, but he always caught them. He would lecture them and then give them slices of honeybread. The whole thing had become a game, a way for them to eat.

A breeze from a far-off sea flowed over the barren hills and cooled Bird's sweaty body. Right ahead, leaning over the road, was a huge old tree. A bandit might be hiding in it. If only the moon were bigger so she could at least see if there was a bandit. All right, if a bandit jumped out of the tree, she would wait until he grabbed her and then bite him—on the face if possible, maybe on the nose.

Her heart cheered at the thought of sinking her teeth into a bandit's fat nose. She was not a booby like children who had parents to cuddle and feed them. She felt sorry for anyone or anything, from bandits to mountain lions, who dared fight her. On the side of the road, she picked up a big stick with a sharp-pointed end. She ran by the tree, stabbing the stick upward. "Umph! Umph!" Her shouts echoed through the barren moonlit hills.

Safely past the tree, she allowed herself to walk again but kept the pointed stick for a walking cane. *Thump, pouf, thump, pouf.* Of course, there were worse things than bandits. Every now and then, somebody in Graynok would disappear, and folk would mutter fearfully about the Analari, giant creatures with dragonfly wings. The Analari flew out of the mountains at night and ate folk, bones and all. If an Analari came, what would she do? Poke it with her stick? An Analari would just laugh at her stick. It would gobble her up like a little cookie.

The road uncoiled, rounding hill after hill. She had never imagined that Farwender lived so far away. It was taking too long to get there; Piper might already be dead. She flung her stick down and began to run, uphill, downhill, uphill, as hard as she could, on and on, until her throat hurt from swallowing dust and breathing hard, until no matter what, she couldn't make herself run more, and yet she ran.

Somewhere deep in the night, half asleep, stumbling along, she found herself on a canyon brink. A light winked far below. She came to life. She leaped down the steep road straight to the light, which turned out to be hanging from the porch post of a hut.

"Farwender!" she shouted, pounding the door. "Farwender!" The door flew open. There was Farwender, standing like a mountain.

"My stars!" boomed Farwender. "It's Bird." He crouched to give her a hug that about crushed her bones. Then he held her back from him and studied her, worriedly. "Calm down. You're safe now. But child, why are you here?"

"Piper's got cat's fever!" Bird cried out, as best she could between gulps of air. "You have to come! Quick!"

Farwender furled his brow. "Twist's child?"

She nodded.

"Just a moment," said Farwender, rising briskly and walking

back into the hut. His beard and long stringy hair were gray, but he wasn't old. He began to rummage hurriedly through the heaps of dried herbs and parchment rolls that covered the table. More piles were mounded on several chairs and stools and most of the floor.

Now what is Farwender up to? Bird wondered, when suddenly, out of a dark corner of the hut, a huge animal appeared and gave her face a big, gooey lick. She screamed and jumped back. Its head looked like a lion's, but its body was like a shaggy dog's, covered with black and white spots.

"What is it?" she asked uneasily. The animal looked at her with mild, golden eyes.

"That's Ally," said Farwender. "He's a chimera. Don't be afraid. He won't bite you, not with either of his mouths."

"Mouths?" said Bird, puzzled. All at once a long, thick, green snake wrapped itself around her neck and flicked its tongue against her cheek. She yelped.

"Don't worry," said Farwender, dumping a basket of yarn on the floor and furiously digging through it. "That's just Ally's tail. He's trying to be friendly. Could you help me? There's something I absolutely must find: a tiny vial, cut glass, glimmers like a star. I can't believe I lost it."

Bird unwound Ally's snake tail from her neck. "Forget the vial. We have to go. Right now. Piper might die."

"I understand that," said Farwender, sounding irritated with himself. "But there's no point in going without it. Why don't I keep better track?" He plowed through a stack of carrots and knitted hats on a chair, disturbing the nap of a white kitten, which pounced to the floor and began to stalk a red and yellow sock.

"Oho!" cried Farwender. "Of course!"

Bird saw a flash of light as Farwender took a small something from the sock and stowed it in the recesses of his robe. Then he scooped up the kitten and kissed its nose. "I name you Finder," he said, and packed the kitten in his robe as well.

Bird wanted to yell at him. This was no time to be naming a kitten. But at last Farwender actually seemed ready to leave. "Time is wasting," he said. "Would you mind if I carry you? For speed?"

"Please!" she cried.

Farwender put a sling over his shoulder and helped her climb into it, so it held her piggyback. "Could you tuck this in somewhere?" he asked, handing her a crock of honey and a chunk of bread. He turned to the chimera. "I'd like you to come too, Ally. The hills host much wickedness at this hour." Finally, to Bird's great relief, Farwender took up his long wooden staff and plunged running into the night, with Ally galloping at his side.

Bird was amazed at Farwender's speed. They would be in Graynok in no time. Who cared about mountain lions or bandits or Analari? Ally could bite them with both his mouths. Farwender would give Piper the glimmering medicine and she would be saved. They would have a feast of honeybread, and Piper would race through the streets again, as she loved to do, holding her tiny arms out from her sides like wings. But would they be too late? Was Piper already gone? The darkness flowed softly over Bird, whispering questions without answers.

BIRD awoke to the stone houses of Graynok rising all around, and Farwender speaking her name. The moon was still high in the sky, as if only moments had passed since they left Farwender's hut.

2

THE THALASSE

Thalasse—Sacred oil of the northern peoples, particularly the Wenish, distilled from the sap of a rare native Wenish tree. Fragrant, phosphorescent. Used in rites surrounding birth, death, coming of age, community feasting, personal distress, war, and the like. Usually applied to the forehead, where it leaves a shining spot sometimes called the Holder's touch.

—*HOREN'S HERBAL LORE*

BIRD knew the lordhouse well, even in the dark. She ran up the curling stone staircase straight to Piper's room, leaving Farwender and Ally to follow along as best they could. She burst through the door curtain and then stopped. Twist sat holding Piper upright against her shoulder, rocking her in the darkness. Their heads were silhouetted in the moonlight coming through the window, Piper's hair-tuft a small flag atop her head. It was so silent that for a moment Bird was sure she had come too late. But then she heard Piper's gasp, with the crying sound of baby kittens in it that gave cat's fever its name.

"Bird," said Twist in a tired voice, "where did you go?"

Bird suddenly remembered that Twist was suspicious of Farwender, because he wasn't from Graynok and because he acted far too nice to everybody for no reason. She said carefully, "I brought Farwender. He has some special medicine he thinks might help."

Twist turned her lean, pocked face to look out the window toward the moon. "You know I have no money," she said bitterly. "If I did, I would get a true doctor, not him."

Just then, Farwender came through the door curtain, with Ally right behind. "Get that horrible animal out of here!" Twist screamed. At Farwender's signal, the chimera slipped away. The big man moved from the shadows to kneel in front of Twist, bringing his rough face into the moonlight. He drew the glowing vial from the recesses of his robe and held it out in the palm of his thick hand. The stone room filled with its soft silvery light. "The thalasse," he said quietly. "The gift of the Holder. It has healed many."

"Ha!" said Twist. "I don't believe you. You just want my money."

"The thalasse costs more than anyone could ever pay, and so there is no charge," said Farwender.

"Don't you dare touch my baby," said Twist.

Bird's insides tightened. "Couldn't we give her just a tiny bit? A true doctor couldn't help now. Don't be a ninny."

Twist shook her head.

There was a long silence, during which Piper, working her mouth like a caught fish, managed to take one more breath. "Come on, Twist," Bird pleaded. "Pretty soon it'll be too late."

Twist shook her head again. The silence thickened. Piper struggled on, but she couldn't seem to get any more air. Bird herself could scarcely breathe. Piper's head made crazy little jerks, and her movements became slower, feebler.

Twist lowered the child, holding Piper flat in the bed of her arms. Bird thought Farwender would give Piper a few drops to drink, but instead, he tipped the vial onto his finger and rubbed a shiny spot on Piper's forehead. He said, "Piper, receive the touch of the Holder."

They all held still and listened. Piper gasped, then struggled, and then her little body sagged into lifelessness.

"No," moaned Twist, hugging the child back to herself. She glared at Farwender. "You've killed her. Get out of here."

"Patience," said Farwender.

"Let me hold her," begged Bird.

"Never," said Twist, and began to sob.

Then all at once, in the net of Twist's arms, Piper began to squirm. She gave a wheezing gasp, and then another that was easier and longer. Then her breathing quieted and became regular, as if nothing had ever been the matter. When Piper began a whistling snore, they all laughed.

"It worked." Twist's voice was new and soft. She cuddled Piper and crooned, "Mama's little fig."

"See, I told you it would work," said Bird, wishing she could cuddle Piper too.

Twist bedded Piper down on her straw bed, being careful not to wake her. The spot where Farwender had rubbed the thalasse kept shining like a promise. When Bird kissed her cheek, Piper's blue eyes popped open. "Bid," she said, and then fell back asleep.

Since Piper didn't need the gold-stitched blanket anymore, Bird took it back. As she was folding it to fit into her pocket,

Farwender asked to see it. He brought it near the thalasse light.

"Where did you get this?" A hint of suspicion darkened his voice.

"I didn't steal it," said Bird. "It's my star blanket. My mother made it. She wrapped me in it on the day I was born, Old Hunch said. It used to be bigger, but now it's all worn away." A familiar sadness, her father-wanting feeling, pressed against her chest. Someday, her father would come searching for her. He would know she was his daughter when he saw the star blanket.

Farwender studied the blanket's gold embroidery as if to read it like a letter, then looked at Bird's face as if to read that too. "Tell me about your mother."

"Old Hunch said she was as beautiful as a wild poppy. She came to the market with me wrapped in this blanket and begged Old Hunch for shelter, just for one night. But that night, she died. Then Old Hunch took care of me."

"Do you know your mother's name?"

"Nope."

"And your father?"

"Old Hunch didn't know anything about him." Bird's father-wanting sadness pressed so hard that she could only whisper. She needed the blanket back. She reached for it.

"Quite curious," Farwender mused, ignoring her reaching. "It seems half of a whole. Look how this border of stars goes around three sides, but the fourth side has a sort of medallion of birds, which has been cut right down the middle."

Yes, she thought, I know, and my father has the other half. "Give it here."

Farwender looked again at Bird, as if he finally understood something. He folded the star blanket as carefully as if it were his own and gave it back to her. She slipped it into her pocket and took a deep breath.

Farwender went to his sling, fished out the honey and bread, and commenced to prepare a snack. Twist allowed Ally back in the room, but she insisted that the chimera stay as far away from her as possible. She couldn't get used to Ally's snake tail, especially after Farwender told her it was a venomous snake.

Everybody feasted on honeybread, including Ally, for chimeras love anything with honey on it. Bird sat leaning against Ally, so he wouldn't feel too unwelcome, and from time to time scratched his ears, which were velvety soft. Farwender brought Finder, the white kitten, out of his robe in case she wanted honeybread too, but she wasn't interested.

"About the medicine," Twist told Farwender as she licked every bit of honey from her skinny fingers. "When I get some money, I'll pay you something."

Farwender handed Twist another slice of honeybread. "You can pay me this way: Don't tell anyone about the thalasse. It could mean my death, and yours as well."

Mistrust closed down Twist's face. "Why?"

"The more I tell you, the more danger for us all. Suffice to say there are those who would pay great sums to know this vial of thalasse exists, and that I am its keeper." Ally, questing for more honeybread, nudged Farwender's arm. "For that matter,"

Farwender said, feeding his chimera, "don't mention Ally either. He's not commonly believed to exist."

He regarded Twist grimly. "Please promise me your silence."

Twist looked away, but nodded yes.

"You too, Bird," said Farwender.

"I promise," Bird said as best she could with her mouth crammed with honeybread.

Too soon it was time for Farwender to go. He tucked the kitten back into his robe. When he packed away the thalasse, the room went dark, except for the shining spot on Piper's forehead. "Bird? Would you see me out?" Farwender asked. "There's something we need to talk about."

They made their way through the unlit house and out into the stone street, where they sat on a low wall that overlooked the dark town. The wide-grin moon hung low in the sky. Ally stayed on alert, positioning himself between Bird and Farwender, his lion's eyes scanning the town below, his snake's eyes watching the street and the lordhouse where Bird lived.

Farwender said, "I might be able to find out some information about your star blanket."

"How?" Bird asked, her voice tight with yearning.

"The embroidery on your blanket was done by my people, the Wenish. I've never seen it done in gold—usually it's colorful cottons—but I'm sure it's Wenish. I'm going to Wen, and I could ask around. I wouldn't need to take your blanket. I've got a good memory for patterns, from knitting."

Bird leaped from the wall. An adventure with Ally and Farwender to find her father! "I'll go with you!" she cried quietly, being careful not to wake anybody up. Folk might throw things out their windows.

"Listen. I don't want you to get your hopes too high. Much of the war has been in Wen. So much has been lost." He bowed his head. "So many have died."

Was her father dead? "When are we leaving?"

Farwender heaved his broad shoulders as if shifting a burden. "Much as I would enjoy your company, I must go alone. It's a long, dangerous trip, at least a moon, over the mountains and beyond. I was going to come to market tomorrow to tell you. Now I've seen you, I can leave tonight."

"But I'm a good fighter. I came all the way to your house by myself."

"A brave deed. But there's no need for you to risk yourself again."

"Oh snot." Bird plunked herself back down on the wall. "Then I'll go by myself." She burrowed her bare feet into Ally's mane. Suddenly she sat straight up. "I'll make you a deal. I'll stay here if you give me some of that thalasse." She would put some on the little blind boy. She'd sell the rest for traveling funds.

Farwender took a deep breath and looked up at the stars. "I should explain. The thalasse isn't a medicine. I didn't even know for sure that it would heal Piper. It was just a good guess and all I knew to do." He thought for a moment. "I suppose you could say the thalasse is pure goodness. When it touches you, some of that goodness flows into you, and fixes you up a bit. You might be healed, like Piper, but it does other things too, things that are harder to put your finger on. It might help you love someone you hate, or maybe tell you something important you need to do. It's totally unpredictable. Sometimes folk are disappointed, or mad, after they experience it, because it doesn't do what they want."

"Could you put some thalasse on me, to see what would happen?" Bird smiled at Farwender, her smile that usually made him give her what she wanted.

Farwender shook his head. "I wish I could. But this is all that remains in the whole world. I have to save it for emergencies."

"Can't you get more?"

"The thalasse is made from the sap of a tree that was the only one of its kind in the world. Now it's gone. Someday there'll be a new tree. Then you can have some. I shall personally see to it."

"But I want some now," she said, kicking her heels against the wall they sat on. She was sure Farwender could spare a tiny bit.

His voice hardened. "I said no. None now. And while I am gone, I want you to promise me that you will stop stealing. I know you think you are the best thief in Graynok, but even the best get caught. Lord Rendarren is tightening his rule, and his justice is fast and cruel. A child younger than you lost her nose over at High Hamlet Market, just the other day. All she did was steal a loaf of bread."

Bird glowered up at him. "You're not my father. You can't tell me what to do," she said. But Farwender's words made her stomach go twitchy. When Lord Rendarren's armies had ravaged Graynok a few years past, his soldiers had sliced the heads off dogs, babies, and old women, which was how Old Hunch had died.

"Which brings me to my main purpose," said Farwender. "I would like to ask a special favor of you. While I am gone, it would give me great peace of mind if you would agree to live with a friend of mine. Her name is Soladin. She sets an excellent table—fresh cheese, lemonade, pies, ham."

Bird's mouth watered at the mention of ham. She had only tasted it once—stolen—but she still dreamed of its salty, smoky flesh. "Where does she live?"

"Near me on the river. Her beds are warm and soft. She could use help harvesting her garden."

"Would she beat me?"

"Never."

"Can Twist and Piper come?"

Farwender nodded. "If Twist wants to."

Hooray, Bird thought. I'll steal money from Soladin and follow Farwender. She crossed her arms over her chest. "I'll think about it."

Farwender stood up. He seemed tired and worried. "Let's go."

SOON Bird was again in Farwender's backsling, going to Soladin's house. Farwender was striding, not running, as he had earlier that night to reach Piper in time. Ally pranced at his side, his white-and-black-spotted body eerie in the moonlight. Twist had chosen to stay behind, still suspicious of Farwender, for all the wonder of Piper's healing.

"Why do we have to keep the thalasse a secret?" Bird asked

as she joggled along on Farwender's back, watching Ally's snake tail swing back and forth. "Who would pay lots of gold to know about you and the thalasse?"

"Lord Rendarren. It's a long story."

"I want to hear it." Maybe he would explain about the long scar on his chest, and about having a chimera.

"This is not the time to tell it. Later. I promise."

The wide-grin moon set behind the barren hills. Bird slept.

3

A Beautiful, Sad Woman

Although she was hardly past girlhood, and looked as fragile as a butterfly, Soladin was the most powerful person in all of Wen, for she was Treekeeper, and wore the Key and the Seed. She was also the most beautiful woman in Wen, graceful and quick, dashing about with her long moonpale hair flying after like a silken banner. At least, such was the opinion of Farwender, the young and newly mantled Watchman of Wen, famous already for his sharp eyes and wisdom. Like all of Wen, he loved Soladin, and in the end, his love proved stronger and more enduring than love usually does.

—*A HISTORY OF WEN,* BY ISOGOLDE OF GILLADOOR

"WE'RE here," said Farwender. He knelt to let Bird climb from his backsling. The porch lantern revealed a cottage with pots of ruffled flowers near the door. A dark forest grew all around and the Rilla Nilla River rushed loudly close by.

"I don't want to live here. I've changed my mind. I'm going with you," said Bird, sleepy and grumpy.

"Not possible," said Farwender. "As I explained. But you could help me out. I need someone to take care of Ally. I can tell he already considers you his special friend. Soladin will help you feed him. He likes to sleep in the middle of the bed. I hope that's all right with you."

Bird scowled and dug all her fingers into Ally's thick mane. Ally pushed his head against her fingers in pleasure.

Farwender reached into his robe and drew out the white kitten. "It comes to me I've been entirely unrealistic, thinking I had room in my life for a cat. Would you like Finder for your own?"

"Sure," said Bird. She didn't know what else to say. There was no keeping Farwender, she could tell that much. She nestled the sleepy kitten in her arms. Farwender banged on the door and boomed, "Soladin! Soladin!" in a voice loud enough to fell a tree.

No one answered, but through the windows Bird saw a light moving in the cottage, and soon a tall, willowy woman holding a candle answered the door, the most beautiful and saddest-looking woman Bird had ever seen.

"Milady Soladin," said Farwender solemnly, bowing his head.

"You're beautiful!" Bird burst out.

"So I have been told," said Soladin in a feathery melancholy voice, as if being beautiful were a great tragedy. "And whom have I the pleasure of meeting?" Her eyes were pools of sorrow in her perfect, stern face.

"This is Bird," said Farwender, "a brave and noble orphan of Graynok, who has this night placed herself under our protection. Bird, I present to you the Lady Soladin."

"Welcome, Bird of Graynok," said Soladin. "My home is yours." Bird noticed that Soladin spoke with Farwender's accent, giving words a hushed, cooing sound instead of the flat speaking of Graynok folk.

Farwender took a step back. "And now, I bid you farewell. I shall miss you both enormously."

"Must you risk your life again for nothing?" said Soladin. "Please don't go, on my account if for no other reason. It will only be the same disappointments." The worry on Soladin's face made Bird afraid.

"Peace, Soladin, there is no other choice," said Farwender gently. "Bird has agreed to tend Ally, and to take on the white kitten as her own."

"But you always take Ally with you, for protection," said Soladin.

"I've changed my mind. Rendarren's power grows. I need most to be unnoticed, which is hard enough, given my bulk. Ally makes it impossible."

"The kitten's name is Finder," Bird told Soladin. "Ally will sleep with me."

Soladin sighed. "So it shall be."

Then Bird witnessed a great love pass between Farwender and Soladin, not an embrace, but a long drinking look into each other's eyes. This ended abruptly when Farwender drew the thalasse vial from his robe. "And then there is this. Could I trouble you to keep a bit here?"

Soladin's face tightened.

Farwender continued. "I understand how you feel, but if anything should happen to me, it would be a true comfort to know there was still some thalasse in the world."

"How can you even ask?" said Soladin coldly. She turned abruptly and went back into the cottage.

"What's going on?" Bird asked.

Farwender put the thalasse vial back inside his robe and crouched down to her size. "Why is Soladin so sad?" she whispered. "Is she always like that? Why does she hate the thalasse?"

"Yes, she is always sad," said Farwender, looking rather sad himself. "Or at least, almost always. It's about something that happened long ago, which I have no business telling you. Don't feel bad if you can't make her happy. Her sorrow is past the mending of time or friendship, mine or yours. Sometimes she becomes especially sad, and then you must treat her gently and give her time to be alone."

When Bird saw the tenderness in Farwender's dark eyes, she yearned to journey with him more than ever. "Please, can I go with you?" she begged.

Farwender's eyes changed from gentle to fierce. "You are not, for any reason, to follow me. Please honor our friendship by respecting my wishes." His words burned into her heart like the command of a king. She nodded yes, even though she had no intention of obeying him.

Farwender stood. His voice returned to its usual friendly rumble. "Take heart. I will inquire about your star blanket." He scratched Ally's and Finder's heads, gave Bird's shoulder a squeeze, and strode off into the forest. Again her father-wanting pushed against her chest. She held her star blanket for a few moments before she walked into Soladin's cottage.

Bird could hardly believe what she saw inside. On a long table before the fire, Soladin had spread a feast, more food than Bird had ever seen for one meal—bread, cheese, walnut meats, a basket of apples, a mug of milk, and a great lump of ham.

"I thought Finder might like her milk warmed," said Soladin, pulling a small bowl from the fire. Bird put the white kitten near the milk. Ally went to work on a bigger bowl filled with a mishmash of foods. At Soladin's direction, Bird washed up at the kitchen pump, and then sat down to eat. Soladin seated herself across the table and began to stab quick stitches into blue cloth.

As Bird glugged down milk, she slid her thief's eyes over the room. Floor-to-ceiling shelves were stocked with crocks and jugs, sacks and baskets. The fireplace took up a whole wall. Soladin was rich. Where did she hide her money?

Bird crammed her mouth with ham and asked, "Is Farwender your boyfriend? Are you afraid he's going to die?"

Soladin lifted her hand. "I dislike the sight of people talking with their mouths full."

Bird swallowed and again asked her questions.

Soladin lifted her hand again. "I also dislike idle chatter."

Bird stopped talking. She ate as much as she could as fast as she could, which was hard because she had eaten so much honeybread already that night. She slipped a handful of nuts into her tunic pocket when Soladin wasn't looking, to start her journey stash.

When Bird finished eating, Soladin had her wash up again. Then she led Bird upstairs to a tiny room with a bed, gave her a nightgown of about the right size, told her to change into it, and left.

With her clean face and nightgown, Bird felt like a rich princess. The bed was warmer and softer than anything she had ever known. As she did every night, she spread her star blanket where her head would lie, so she could feel it against her face. Ally, true to Farwender's prediction, took up the bed's middle, leaving her and Finder to arrange themselves around him as best they could.

She snuggled against Ally's vast white-and-black-spotted back and breathed in the ripe sweaty smell of chimera. She hoped her father would be strong and kind like Farwender, but much handsomer. Soladin seemed secretive and smart, the sort of person who would be good at hiding treasure. Maybe there were gold coins in a flour sack, or under a loose stone in the big fireplace.

A lush and unfamiliar sense of safety swept Bird outward into sleep. Her last thought was of Piper, and the blissful smile that had played on the corners of Piper's mouth just after Farwender rubbed her forehead with thalasse.

4

MORE ORPHANS

I was shocked to find the wildling Bird at my door that night, for the way from Graynok is long and perilous. I knew that cat's fever rarely spares its victims and that Piper, Bird's two-year-old ragamuffin friend, would be dead by morning. I determined to save Piper with the thalasse if I could, even though there remains but a thimbleful in the world. With Bird in my backsling, I ran through the hills for Graynok, glad after all my defeats that I could do at least this one small good for my friend Bird, who has often warmed my heart with her fierceness and love.

—*FARWENDER'S REPORT TO THE COUNCIL OF WEN*

BIRD woke in a small white room filled with sunlight, leaf shadows, and a nutty-steamy smell. Ally and Finder were up and gone. Her old raggedy clothes had been taken away and a new pink tunic and blue leggings left in their place. The tunic had ruffles at the shoulders and strawberries embroidered on the yoke. On the floor were short soft boots that tied with thongs. She dressed quickly, feeling stiffly fancy in the new clothes. She folded and pocketed her star blanket and ran downstairs to the kitchen. At the table, she was surprised to discover three children, two boys and a girl, all about her age. All three stopped talking and stared at her as she entered the room.

The light-haired boy whispered, "She's pretty, or at least her face is, where she's clean."

The dark-haired boy whispered back, "No she isn't." All three children giggled, and Bird felt suddenly shy.

Soladin, stirring a pot at the hearth, turned and nailed all the children with her eyes. "Enough," she said. "Children, this is Bird, the new girl I told you about. Please introduce yourselves and help her feel at home."

The boy who said she was pretty was named Dren and the boy who disagreed, Stoke. They said their real names were Pellendren and Brynstoke, but no one ever called them that.

The girl was called Issie for Isogolde. Issie told Bird, "We're orphans, just like you."

"I'm not an orphan," said Bird. "My father is still alive." She walked over to the low window where Ally kept guard to let him wash her face with his big slobbery tongue, a refreshing way to start the day. Right away Soladin said, "Stop that at once. You never know what a chimera has been eating. Please wash your face and hands immediately."

The boys sat together on one side of the table. Stoke had straight black hair that fell over his forehead and double-dark eyes, which Bird found unsettling. He seemed to see straight into her heart. Dren's tawny hair stuck up in the back, and his ears poked out. He appeared to be taller than she was, but skinny, probably easy to beat in a fight. Issie was sunny-looking, with loose curly hair the color of butter. Her round blue eyes gave her an amazed expression, as if she couldn't believe what she was seeing. Bird thought she looked fake. Issie sat opposite the boys, and had Finder curled in her lap.

After Bird washed her hands and face under Soladin's supervision, she sat down next to Issie. "That's my kitten you've got on your lap," Bird told her, "but I'll let you hold her for now. Farwender gave her to me. Her name is Finder."

Issie turned to Soladin. "How come she gets a kitten and I don't? I've always wanted a kitten, forever and ever."

Soladin fed another log to the fire. "People who expect fairness in this life will be sorely disappointed."

Bird smiled at Issie and gave Finder's small white head a hello pat. Issie gave Bird a dirty look. Next Bird smiled at Stoke, and when he smiled back, she kicked him under the table, hard. When he glared at her, she whispered, "I'm going to bite you really hard when you least expect it," and smiled at him again.

"This is for you, Bird. Oatmeal and raisins." Soladin placed a steaming bowl on the table. "Goat's milk and brown sugar are right in front of you. Please limit yourself to one spoon of sugar." Bird flooded her oatmeal with goat's milk, added the biggest spoonful of brown sugar she could scoop, and took a bite. Delicious. She scarcely could believe she was actually eating her third large good-tasting meal in a row.

Soon the other children, accompanied by Ally, left to work in the garden, and Soladin began the washing up. Bird, now with Finder in her lap, continued eating bowls of oatmeal, each topped with the biggest spoonful of brown sugar possible.

"Save some room for lunch," said Soladin, as her dishrag skirted Bird's bowl. Bird swallowed the last mouthful of her fourth serving of oatmeal, then picked up the bowl with both hands and drank down the remaining goat's milk, sweet with brown sugar. She yearned to eat a spoonful of brown sugar straight from the sugar bowl, but she reckoned Soladin would get mad, so she held back.

"More oatmeal?" asked Soladin.

"Nope."

"When someone offers you something and you don't want it, the polite response is 'No, thank you,'" said Soladin. In the morning light, Soladin seemed less strange and sad, more like a normal person, but still very beautiful. She wore her silver-honey hair in a thick braid that circled her head like a crown. She never ceased working—drying dishes, swabbing the floor, throwing scraps out the door to the chickens. Her blue eyes held a look that said, "I am watching you, and I suspect you are not up to my standards."

Bird decided to impress Soladin by being unbelievably obedient, even though she thought Soladin's rules were stupid. "No, thank you, Soladin," she said. "My, that was good, though. Thank you for breakfast, and for the new clothes, and all the food last night, and the bed. It was the softest, warmest bed I ever slept in."

"You are welcome for all of it. I am happy to have you with us," said Soladin in her cool feathery voice. Then she brought her face close to Bird's, looked her directly in the eyes, and said, "I will not abide fighting in this house. If I catch you fighting, I'll send you straight back to Graynok. Fighting includes biting. Do I make myself perfectly clear?"

"Yes, ma'am," said Bird, to calm Soladin down, but of course she would have to fight Stoke, to show him who was boss.

"What happened to my old clothes, ma'am?" Bird asked.

"I burned them. You need a bath. You appear to have never taken one before. The tub is in the next room. Please follow me."

"Yes, ma'am."

Bird liked to be clean and sometimes tried to wash with a cup of water and a rag. But she hadn't taken a hot bath with soap since Old Hunch died. And although her face was clean, because Soladin had made her wash it three times already, her hair was stiff with grease and she smelled like a dead rat. The tub was waist-high and steamed like a soup pot. "It's too hot," Bird said.

Soladin rolled up her tunic sleeves and dipped an elbow into the water. "Nonsense. It's just right. Feel for yourself."

Bird reached her fingers through a thick creamy blanket of bubbles. The water was deliciously warm and lavender-scented. She slipped off her clothes, climbed into the tub, and sat down. The water came up to her chin. Soladin scrubbed her with a soapy cloth, and then washed her hair, rubbing Bird's scalp hard with her fingertips and rinsing with something that smelled again of lavender and made all the snarls untangle. While Soladin dried Bird with a large thick cloth, Bird described how Farwender had healed Piper with the thalasse.

Soladin stopped rubbing. "Oh Farwender! But how can I condemn your generous heart! Bird, listen to me—you must never, ever mention the thalasse to anyone. It could mean the death of all of us, yourself included. Especially Farwender. Do you understand?"

"Don't worry. I already promised Farwender." Bird swiped

her fingers through Soladin's apron pockets. Empty. "Have you ever had the thalasse rubbed on you?"

Soladin pulled Bird's tunic down over her head quick as a leaping squirrel. "I just told you not to talk about the thalasse. If you mention it again, I shall be irritated beyond measure. Now, I just love your shiny black hair. How shall we fix it?"

"Just like yours." She wanted to look as much like Soladin as possible.

It took most of the morning for Soladin to fix Bird's hair, because she was determined to first remove each and every louse nit. Finally she finished. "You look lovely." She handed Bird a mirror. "See for yourself."

Bird had seen her face a few times in puddles and dark windows. Still, it was a shock to see herself now, so clearly, so clean, a small pale face with slanted dark eyes, shiny like watermelon seeds, framed with a tidy circlet of black braids.

For the first time in her life, Bird thought, I do look pretty. Not beautiful like Soladin, but at least pretty. She wished Piper and Twist could see her, and everybody in Graynok, and Farwender. And Stoke.

"The morning vanishes," said Soladin. "Come along to the garden."

5

The Fight

Each new moon, Soladin came to the altar in the forest, to Far-
wender, the Watchman of Wen, that he might anoint her with
thalasse, that she might guard the Tree with wisdom and strength
beyond her own. But a new moon came when Soladin did not
appear. All day, Farwender waited for her. As night fell, there at
last she was. She came to the altar, but did not kneel or give the
customary greetings. Instead she said, all in a rush, "Farwender,
dearest love, I must beg a great favor."

He nodded, already afraid of what this might be.

Soladin lowered her eyes. "Could we skip the thalasse, just
this once, and not tell anybody?"

Farwender was stunned. For Soladin not to submit to the tha-
lasse was a great betrayal of her people, an offense beyond mur-
der among the Wenfolk, punishable by banishment. For him not
to tell of it was likewise.

—*A HISTORY OF WEN,* BY ISOGOLDE OF GILLADOOR

WITH Finder the kitten leaping this way and that in front of
them, Bird and Soladin walked to the garden, which was
planted near the cottage in a clearing along the Rilla Nilla
River. In the rich river-bottom soil, Soladin grew every manner of vegetable, some fruits, winter fodder—mostly mangle
root for Farwender's sheep—and herbs for cooking, scent, and

healing. It was now late summer, and the garden was thick with cornstalks, beans on poles, giant pumpkins, and zucchini the size of stove wood.

As Bird stepped from the forest shade into the vegetable patch, she felt someone's eyes on her. She looked up and was pleased to see that the eyes belonged to Stoke. At her glance, Stoke looked away. He was pushing a barrow loaded with carrots, coming toward them, and soon all met. "Stoke, please show Bird what to do," asked Soladin, and strode back toward the cottage, her long overtunic billowing behind her.

Bird and Stoke eyed each other. Bird had an urge to take off her straw hat, so Stoke might see her crown of braids.

Stoke said, "I'm sorry for what I said at breakfast." These were the first words he ever spoke directly to Bird. It was also the first time in Bird's life anyone had ever apologized to her. She found it unsettling. Stoke's dark eyes were so raw and true that she looked away.

"I mean it," Stoke said.

"So?"

"So do you forgive me?"

"I'll think about it." She was still mad about what he had said. Maybe tomorrow she would forgive him. She snapped her teeth at him, like a dog, to remind him of her promise to bite him.

"Have it your way," he mumbled. "Go to Issie. Let her show you what to do." Bird watched him go, struck by his square shoulders and straight back. He pushed his wheelbarrow of carrots like a warrior.

The carrots grew in a green ferny stripe about a cart's breadth wide and a hundred paces long. Bird couldn't imagine why Soladin wanted so many carrots. Issie had Bird help her pull and stack. Dren worked ahead of them, loosening the earth with a digging fork. Close by, the Rilla Nilla poured noisily over sun-warmed rocks into a deep pool. The cotton-wood leaves shushed and wasps nibbled the river mud.

As they worked, Issie chattered. Bird didn't listen much, because she kept thinking of Stoke, seeing his dark eyes and his black straight hair that flopped over his forehead. She couldn't decide if she wanted to be his worst enemy or best friend.

"Which one do you think is handsomer, Stoke or Dren?" asked Issie. Bird didn't answer. "Well, in my opinion, Stoke is handsomer but Dren is more fun. Stoke is so serious. He's hard to talk to. It was funny he made that joke about you at break-fast. He never makes jokes. He must like you. I've lived with Soladin since I was two. I was her first orphan. Farwender found me in the high mountains, sitting on a big boulder. I was eating peppermints. My face was all sticky with peppermint drool and when Farwender came up, I offered him a pepper-mint, my last one. I had a note pinned to my tunic that said my parents were dead, so would somebody please take pity on me. Farwender brought me to Soladin to keep her company, to keep her mind off things. Pretty soon he brought Dren and Stoke too, so we've all been together for years and years just like a family. Except I've always wanted a sister. Now you're here. It's so special to have a sister."

"I brought some money with me," Bird interrupted. "Do you know a good place where I can hide it?"

"I think Soladin has lots of gold hidden somewhere, but I don't know where. She doesn't like to burden us with secrets.

I'm sure she wouldn't mind putting your money in the same place. Do you have your money with you now? Can I see it?"

"I left it in my room. I don't like to show it to people."

THE day was hot, and before their midday meal, Bird and the other orphans splashed in the Rilla Nilla. They ate sitting on boulders in the shade of a big oak, which overhung the river. A breeze cooled their wet faces and bodies. Bird rested against Ally's back and let Issie hold Finder again. She liked Issie. As Bird fed a bit of cheese to Ally's snake tail, she wondered what Twist and Piper had found to eat this day.

"So how do you like pulling carrots?" asked Stoke.

"I don't," said Bird. "So what's the name of the town Farwender went to?"

"We're not supposed to talk about where Farwender goes," Stoke answered in a friendly way. "Soladin's rules. What can you tell us about Graynok? None of us has ever been there. I think Soladin's afraid of the place."

"Graynok's a broken-down mess, thanks to Rendarren." Bird squinted her eyes against the sun flashing off the river. She took a big crisp bite of apple. "Last night Farwender put some thalasse on my forehead, just for fun. Have any of you ever had thalasse on you?"

Issie gave Bird a patient look. "We're not supposed to talk about that either. Soladin's rules."

"Soladin sure has piles of rules," Bird said. "I don't suppose you ever break them."

The other children shifted uncomfortably. Dren said, "Not unless we want to go without dinner." Issie giggled.

"They're good rules," said Stoke. He rose, brushing off sand. "Back to work."

THE afternoon burned hotter and hotter, and Bird's thoughts got hotter too, as she brooded on how Stoke had said she wasn't pretty, and how nobody would answer her questions. Pulling carrots was hard, boring work. Her body dripped sweat. Finally, to amuse herself, after checking to make sure Issie and Dren weren't watching, Bird picked up a small rock and threw it hard at Stoke's back. It hit his head. He turned to see where it came from, rubbing the sore spot. Bird was already back pulling carrots.

Thrilled at her daring and good aim, Bird kept whizzing rocks at Stoke at every chance, but she soon became frustrated. Stoke was ignoring her. He didn't even rub where the rocks hit anymore, or turn around to see who might be throwing them.

Next time Stoke barrowed by, Bird stuck out her foot and tripped him. He sprawled face first into the ferny carrot plants. Before he could get up, Bird jumped him and boxed his ears. She knew from personal experience this really hurt. Stoke struggled out from under her, pushed her into the carrots face-down, and pinned her shoulders with both hands. "Promise to stop throwing rocks at me and I'll let you up," he said calmly.

"I promise," Bird said, but when Stoke released her, she sprang to her feet and again tackled him down. She felt powerful, gleeful, even though Stoke was stronger and almost twice her weight. She loved fighting. But then, to her dismay, lickety-split, he clinched his arms around her and stood up, pulling her with him. He snatched one of her arms and winched it behind her back. He had won, just like that. Dren and Issie were looking on, staring.

"I'll get Soladin," said Dren, starting toward the cottage. Now Soladin would kick her out. Suddenly, too late, Bird was filled with regret.

But then Stoke called to Dren, "Stop. Don't."

Dren sat down on a big pumpkin. "She's just going to fight you again, the minute you let go. You can't hold her arm behind her back all day."

"Dren's right," said Issie. "Bird's as wild as a mountain lion. She tripped you and jumped you and tricked you. Wait till Soladin hears about this." Issie picked up Finder and nuzzled her nose-to-nose. "That Bird's going to be kicked out. And then you will be my cat, won't you?"

Stoke kept his grip firm on Bird's arm. "Let's give her another chance. Bird's just getting used to us."

"I don't need any favors from you," said Bird, even though she desperately hoped Issie and Dren would go along with Stoke. She wanted to keep having good food, a warm bed, and steaming baths, but she was embarrassed for the others to know how much she hungered to stay. Besides, she hadn't had time to steal anything yet.

Issie cocked her head to one side, as if she found Bird puzzling. "Bird, do you want to stay or not?"

All the children waited for her answer. Bird swallowed her impulse to spit in their faces and say, "No, never!" Instead she made herself say, "I guess."

Stoke let go of her arm. "One more chance. That's all you

get." Bird gave him a dirty look, but he didn't see it. He was already rolling his carrot wheelbarrow.

"See, Bird?" said Issie. "What did I say? Stoke likes you. Do you like him? You can tell me. We're sisters. I won't tell anyone."

Maybe Issie is right, thought Bird. She'd never had a boyfriend before. It was weird but nice. Still she said to Issie, "Stoke's too much of a goody-goody. Dren is much cuter."

Despite her words, for the rest of the afternoon, Bird's mind reeled with thoughts of Stoke. Sometimes she imagined taking revenge upon him. She would yank a carrot from the earth and pretend it was a handful of his dark hair. Other times she pictured the two of them in battle, fighting back to back, outnumbered a hundred to two and winning.

The children pulled carrots until dinner, and still there were more carrots left in the ground. They smelled like carrots even after they washed up at the pump outside the cottage. Dinner was carrot soup. They ate in the long light of the summer evening and afterward sat at the kitchen table knitting or mending or whittling, because Soladin had a rule about everyone always having busy hands. Stoke and Dren were carving cooking spoons. Stoke's was tiny and lopsided, but Dren's was magnificent, with roses and rosebuds worked on the handle. Issie was crocheting lace for the bottom of her tunic. Farwender had already taught Bird to knit, and so she began a neck scarf for Piper. It would be stripes of different shades of red, Piper's favorite color. Soladin complimented Bird on her even, careful stitches. Soladin was knitting a blanket for Farwender from every color in the world.

As the evening dimmed, Soladin had the children put away their work and sit quietly. "Bird, it is our custom before bed to thank the Holder for all He has done for us this day."

"Who's the Holder?" asked Bird.

"He who made the worlds and stars and everything else," said Soladin. "He who gives us strength in the day and songs in the night. We hear His voice in the babe's cry and the thunder's crack and we see His face in our own faces. Everything good comes from Him."

"Where do all the bad things come from?" asked Bird.

"Rendarren," said Stoke. "Everybody knows that."

"Evil comes from all of us, especially me," said Soladin. "Issie, would you please begin? Show Bird how we give thanks."

Issie closed her eyes. "I thank you, dearest Holder, for my long yellow curly hair." Yuk, thought Bird.

"Thank you, Holder, for my strength," said Stoke. "Please allow me to use it in your service."

"I know lots of people stronger," said Bird. "Me, for example."

"No interrupting," said Soladin.

"Yes, ma'am," said Bird, glad she had put Stoke in his place.

Dren said, "Thank you, Holder, that Issie is afraid of big, hairy spiders."

Issie gave a little shriek. Soladin frowned. "Pellendren. Don't be annoying. Please begin again."

"Yes, ma'am," said Dren. "I thank you, Holder, for bringing Bird to live with us."

"Very nice," said Soladin. "Bird?"

"I'm thankful I don't have long curly yellow hair and I'm stronger than Stoke and I'm not afraid of anything at all," said Bird.

"Bird," said Soladin, "you are not to use our time of thanks for meanness. Please try again."

Was it worth all this trouble for a few meals and a chance to steal some gold? Bird wondered. Then her stomach curdled with memories of how it felt not to eat for a day, or two or three. Feeling Finder's small body on her lap, Bird remembered the time she and Twist had eaten a cat. Bird had done the killing, smashing its head with a rock. The cat had been gray-and-white striped, almost all bones. "I'm thankful for food," she said. "Oatmeal, brown sugar, ham, honeybread, even carrots."

Bird looked at Soladin to see if she approved, but Soladin was gazing out the window with a far-off look on her face. Stoke tapped Soladin on the shoulder. She folded her hands and said in her feathery voice, "I thank you, Holder, Lord of Life, that we are safe another day, that Rendarren has not found us."

AT bedtime, Soladin smoothed the covers over Bird the best she could, considering that Ally was lying in the middle of the bed. There was a sunshine smell of fresh sheets. A cool river wind came through the open window. Soladin leaned over, touched her soft dry lips to Bird's forehead, and said, "I was gathering rose hips near the garden. I saw you pick that fight with Stoke."

"But I—" Bird started, intending to deny everything.

Soladin interrupted, "Hush now. You can stay. Good night. I love you."

Bird heard these last three words in disbelief. No one had ever said "I love you" to her before, although she had sometimes whispered those words to Piper. She felt a wash of comfort and almost answered back, "I love you too," but she didn't. After all, Soladin hadn't known her long. She would wait to see if Soladin really loved her, for days and days, years and years. And she would wait until she was sure she loved Soladin. She had long ago promised herself that she would never say "I love you" to anybody unless she really meant it.

6

The Marking

Then a time came when I no longer wished to experience the tha-lasse. I no longer wanted to know the love of the Holder, but only the love of Rendarren.

—*CONFESSIONS*, BY SOLADIN LEAFSTAR, TREEKEEPER OF WEN

THE last days of summer unfurled like golden ribbons in the wind and blew away. Bit by bit, shelf by shelf, when the others were busy elsewhere, Bird searched for Soladin's gold, inside bags, baskets, crocks, under mattresses and rugs. No luck.

There was always much to do, with the sheep and bees to tend, the housework and harvest. Every day, Bird learned something new: how to bake bread, make cough drops, read and write, swim across the river, fish, make jam, sew with tiny hidden stitches.

Despite the urgency of harvest work, Soladin gave Bird and the others time to play. On hot afternoons, they would ride Ally into the river and try to stay on his back as he swam. Sometimes they would make forts in the blackberry bushes or play hide-and-seek in the river forest. Finder, living up to her name, would discover them in even the most hidden places and announce her accomplishment with howling meows.

Soladin never stopped to play. She was always moving, her strong tanned hands harvesting vegetables, kneading bread, and splitting firewood. In the evening, when everything was clean and ordered for the next day, she would knit before the fire, her needles flashing faster than the river trout when the children tried to grab them. Some days, as Farwender had warned, Soladin was remote and sad. She would hardly speak, and the children could not cheer her. Then she worked harder and faster than ever, but in a forgetful way. She would put forks on the table when they were having soup, and make cookies without sugar.

No matter how she felt, every night Soladin would lead them in thanking the Holder for everything that was: the winking light on the river, Finder's soft fur, how fat the watermelons were growing, the way each blackberry had its own particular taste, the breeze that cooled them as they worked in the hot sun, each other, the crumbly garden soil, and, again and again, that they were safe yet another day, that Rendarren had not found them.

The main thing Bird didn't like was that Stoke was too bossy. She got back at him by secretly putting sand in his food and biting red ants in his bed—just a few, so it would seem a natural occurrence. To her dismay, Stoke never seemed to notice.

Another problem was that sometimes Bird would come across the other orphans huddled, talking in hushed voices. When they saw her, they would break apart and act like nothing was happening. She suspected they were whispering about the thalasse, and where Farwender had gone, and it made her cross that they wouldn't tell her their secrets.

There was always a lot to eat, and Bird shot up taller and stronger. Indeed, with her fresh clothes, tidy braids, and clean face, she appeared an entirely different child. She had never imagined that life could be so free and safe. Sometimes, she felt so safe she even forgot to put her star blanket in her pocket, but left it spread over her pillow. She stopped thinking about running away to find Farwender. Farwender would be back soon enough. She might as well wait.

One late summer afternoon, Soladin was cutting out a winter tunic for Bird from dark purple wool when the scissors slipped from her hand. They landed point down on the stone floor and one blade broke off.

That night over a dessert of apple ping, Stoke asked Soladin, "How can we manage without scissors? Why don't I go to Graynok to get them fixed."

Soladin's face tightened up all over. She looked like an angry fox. "People have managed without scissors in many times and places. It's not worth the risk."

"What risk? Farwender went there all the time. Bird can go with me, to show me around."

"I could take Piper her scarf," said Bird.

Soladin poked holes with her spoon in her apple ping crust.

Stoke said, "We're running out of flour, sugar, and salt. We should stock up before the road gets muddy."

"Good point," said Bird.

"Please stop waving your spoon," said Soladin to Bird.

"Yes ma'am."

"I want to go too," pouted Issie.

"Send all four of us," said Dren. "Then you can have a nice quiet day."

Everybody was paying close attention to Soladin, who had put both hands on her heart and bowed her head. Stealthily, Bird pinched some sand out of her pocket and sprinkled it on Stoke's apple ping.

Stoke put on a grownup-looking face. "Farwender might not be back until spring. We might have to take care of ourselves until then."

Soladin rose from the table and went over to the window, where Ally was, as always, on guard. Or as Bird sometimes thought, watching for Farwender. "All right, I'm tired of arguing. You can go. Just Bird and Stoke," she said in a dull voice.

"Thanks," said Stoke. To Bird's disappointment, Stoke didn't eat any more of his apple ping.

MORNING sunlight touched the hilltops, but the shadows lay deep upon Soladin's cottage in the river canyon. In the pony cart next to Stoke, Bird sat with reins in hand, ignoring all the anxious instructions Soladin was giving her. Instead, Bird was thinking of the basket in the back of the cart, which Soladin had helped her pack the night before. It was full of good things for Twist and Piper: nut cookies, apples, fresh bread, ham, the red-striped scarf Bird had knit for Piper and a larger matching scarf Soladin had knit for Twist. Bird could hardly wait to see Piper's face when she opened the basket. Maybe when Twist tasted the delicious food, she would decide to come live at Soladin's.

Soladin repeated for the hundredth time, "Go carefully but as quickly as possible. Get the scissors fixed, get the flour, sugar, and salt, and come back. You can buy sweets, but be fast about it. Don't talk about Farwender, the thalasse, or me. If you see any of Rendarren's soldiers, come home at once."

"Yes, ma'am," Bird and Stoke chorused.

Farwender had named the pony Apples, so folk would be reminded to give her apples to munch now and again. Bird was to drive Apples to Graynok, Stoke would drive her home. They had drawn straws and she had won. As they wound out of the shadowy river canyon, Bird's heart lifted to feel a brisk wind against her face, and to see castle clouds floating in the blue harvest sky. It was the sort of day that made her think she could fly.

"Why are you always picking on me?" asked Stoke.

"What?"

"The ants, tripping me."

"I never."

"I saw you put the sand in my apple ping last night."

"Prove it."

"I'd like to be friends," said Stoke. "Let's start over. Anyway, whatever you do, I'm not fighting back, because that's Soladin's rules."

"Well, big wody-dody," said Bird, and that was the end of the conversation. She didn't mind the silence. Sometimes it was disgusting to hear Stoke talk.

When Apples pulled the cart into Graynok, Bird sat up straight and proud, but she didn't see anyone she knew. Graynok seemed smaller and more ruined than she remembered. The ancient stone market building, an open hall with dirt floor and arches all around, was half empty and stunk of animal sweat and droppings, old smoke and rancid cooking fats.

Twist and Piper were not in their usual begging place. "We can look for them while we buy things," Stoke suggested. They took the scissors to the tinker, and then bought everything Soladin wanted and loaded it into the pony cart, but still no Twist and Piper. With a sinking feeling, Bird remembered that Twist sometimes missed a day or two of begging.

While Stoke left to pick up the fixed scissors, Bird visited with her friend Chick Lady.

"Where have you been, Bird-child? Where did you get your beautiful garb?" Chick Lady touched the strawberries on Bird's tunic. "Such embroidery. The ruffles on the shoulders are like little wings."

Bird played with the chicks, laughing at their tiny wheeling feet. Too soon, Stoke was back with the scissors. Bird pleaded, "Can't we stay longer? They'll be here any minute. Sometimes Twist sleeps late."

"Soladin already imagines we are dead or worse," said Stoke. "You can choose the sweets."

Even though she knew he would never agree, Bird began to try to convince Stoke to go over to the lordhouse where Twist and Piper lived. She was interrupted by a ruckus of barking dogs, thundering hooves, and people running out of the way, as a troop of soldiers galloped into the square outside the market.

About a dozen riders dismounted and entered the market through an arch several booths away from Bird, Stoke, and Chick Lady. The horsemen were dressed in black from head to toe. Only their eyes showed, glittering through slits in their helmets, which bore swirling goldwork of flowers, spiderwebs, or flames. The gold hilts of daggers stuck out from their sashes and the gold scabbards of curved swords swung in the folds of their robes.

Chick Lady whispered, "It's the Searchers, from Rendarren, come to mark the Wenish. You know, those that are touched with the oil of the Tree. They say three were marked last week at Grassfield Market."

The black-shrouded men were already moving through the market, in pairs, booth by booth. They were systematically laying their black-gloved hands on the head of each man, woman, and child. Everyone held quiet and still, even the babies.

Bird inched closer to Stoke and whispered in his ear. "Did you hear her? It's the Searchers. They do something awful to folk who've had the thalasse rubbed on them."

"I know," said Stoke, barely moving his lips.

"I know you've had it. You better hide quick. Over there, behind those baskets," said Bird.

"They'd see," said Stoke quietly. "It's best to stay absolutely still."

Bird gave Stoke a "you dummy" look. She whispered to Chick Lady, "How do they mark them?"

The woman darted a look toward the approaching black-robed men. She whispered, "It's an X cut into the palm of the hand, with a dagger."

"I've seen it done," Stoke muttered, looking straight ahead, his hands clasped behind his back.

The Searchers hadn't marked anybody yet; at least Bird

hadn't heard anybody scream. Maybe Stoke was the only person in the whole market who had been touched with thalasse. If only Ally were with them. Then they could fight.

Two Searchers arrived at Chick Lady's booth. One of them put his hand on her sparse silver hair, then stood intent and still, as if listening for something hard to hear. A few moments later, apparently satisfied that Chick Lady hadn't been touched with thalasse, the Searcher lifted his hand.

Then the dark-robed men turned their hidden faces toward Bird. The biggest Searcher—he looked even bigger than Farwender—put his black-gloved hand on her head, and immediately an ancient heavy darkness fell upon her. The darkness seemed blacker than the inside of a coffin, after it is sealed and buried forever. It was bigger than the night sky. She felt tiny and naked as a little pink worm. She could see nothing, hear nothing. She wanted to scream and run, or at least clutch her star blanket, but she couldn't move. Then the Searcher's hand lifted and she could see and hear and move again, but she felt as if some of the darkness had been left inside her. She stayed as still and silent as possible, for fear the Searcher would put his hand on her again.

Out of the corner of her eye, Bird watched Stoke. He stood with his chin thrust out, his most grownup look on his face. She was amazed at his courage. He looked the Searcher right in the eyes as the black-gloved hand fell upon him. There was a moment of stillness, and then suddenly, in what seemed a single movement, the man seized Stoke's wrist, pinned his hand to a nearby post, drew a dagger, and cut an X into Stoke's palm.

A gasp swept the market. Stoke didn't cry out, but his face tightened all over in pain. The Searcher rubbed some dark grease into Stoke's palm, and then Stoke screamed, one long cry. He folded his body around his hand. Blood dripped onto his tunic, onto the dirt. The Searchers moved to the next booth.

"Let me see," Bird whispered to Stoke. She was too afraid to speak in a regular voice, with the Searchers so near.

Stoke, shaking, gasping for breath, held out his hand. It was his right hand. There was too much blood to see the cut. Bird grabbed the first thing she could think of—her star blanket—and pressed it hard into Stoke's hand, to stop the blood, as So-ladin had taught her. After a moment she pulled off the cloth, and before the blood welled in the wound again, she saw the awfulness of the cut, deep and careless. She bunched the star blanket back into Stoke's palm.

"Keep the cloth pressed tight against your hand," she said. "You need a doctor."

"No doctor. Soladin can fix it when we get home."

"Then we're going home right now," said Bird.

"We need to buy sweets," said Stoke. "Issie and Dren will be disappointed if we don't buy sweets."

Bird was about to argue when out in the square she saw two familiar figures, Twist and Piper, making their way toward the market. They came slowly, because Piper's legs would go only so fast. With a flush of horror, Bird remembered that Piper had been touched with the thalasse.

The Searchers still worked close by. Bird wanted to stop

Twist and Piper, but she feared to attract the Searchers' attention. Hoping Twist would see her, Bird crept out into the square, as if she hadn't anything particular on her mind. Twist waved. Bird put a terrible grimace on her face and made tiny "go away" swats with her hand. But Twist kept coming with a smile on her face, and now Piper was yelling, "Bid, Bid," and reaching out her hands.

Suddenly, a Searcher swooped down on Piper and clapped his hand on her head. Twist grabbed Piper's arm, to pull her away, but another Searcher laid his hand on her. There was an awful moment when there was nothing but silence, with both Piper and Twist rigid and dumb. Then all at once, a Searcher held Piper's hand against his thigh, cut an X into her palm, and rubbed in the black grease.

Into the utter silence of the market, Piper shrieked with her whole body, holding up a bloody hand. Twist, sobbing, gathered her up and tried to comfort her.

Anger torched Bird's heart. She ran full-speed to her friends. Using her teeth, she ripped two strips of cloth from the bottom of her tunic. She wadded one strip into Piper's hand and quickly tied it in place with the other. Over Piper's wails, Bird shouted into Twist's ear, "I'll go get some medicine—to take away the hurt." Twist, lost in Piper's pain, didn't seem to hear her.

Out in the square, with harsh shouts and pounding hooves, the Searchers were leaving Graynok. Bird dashed to Chick Lady's stall. "I need ointment for Piper, something for the pain. Do you have anything?"

"Leave me be," the woman said.

"Please," said Bird.

Chick Lady spat and gave Bird her back.

"Cheese disease to you too," Bird muttered, and rushed off to the herb woman, who had given her free medicine before. As Bird approached, the herb woman sat down on her stool and pulled her shawl over her head, as if she were taking a nap. Bird ran into the booth, threw back the shawl, and cried into the woman's face, "I need some ointment for pain. Quick. For Piper. The Searchers cut her really bad. I can pay." The herb woman didn't even open her eyes; she acted as if she had been turned to stone.

Piper's unending screams poured through the marketplace. Bird ran breathlessly from booth to booth, asking for ointment, and everywhere folk ignored her, until she knew it was no use. She felt everybody's eyes on her, but when she looked at anyone, they looked away.

Finally Bird sped back to the square. Twist was pacing back and forth, holding the wailing Piper. Bird held out empty hands. "Nobody would give me any medicine. They're all afraid."

Piper reached for Bird, but Twist screamed over Piper's wails, "Don't you dare touch her! You've ruined her. It's all because of you she got the funny oil on her. Now wherever we go, people will hate us."

"Farwender saved her life," yelled Bird.

"Maybe. Maybe not," yelled Twist. She spun from Bird and ran away, her body hunched around Piper. Piper stretched out her arms, screaming Bird's name. Even after Twist crossed the market square and disappeared down a side street, Bird could hear Piper yelling, "Bid, Bid." After Piper's screams faded to nothing, Bird noticed the basket of food and knit scarves, sitting where she had left it, in the corner of Chick Lady's booth.

7
X

Wen is a small but rich and powerful kingdom occupying the entire Oor peninsula. Topography consists in the main of forested hills, which are cleared in their valleys for agriculture. Abundant rain and snow feed an extensive network of streams, collected finally by the Lunashall River as it meanders north to south. The spectacular and nigh impassable Pokadoon Mountains crowd the neck of the peninsula and so sequester Wen from the rest of the world. Wherever one travels in Wen, one is never far from the sea.

—GEOGRAPHY FOR TRAVELERS, BY BACKLANDER

INTO the setting sun the two children traveled; Bird drove to spare Stoke's hand. The dry grass hills, the sky, the castle clouds, and and their own faces turned peach and gold in the sunset light. Stoke's hand had finally stopped bleeding, leaving on his palm two dark red ditches that crossed in a lopsided X.

The darkness that had filled Bird's mind and body when the Searcher laid his hand upon her kept coming back, like nausea from eating bad food. She wished she could hold her star blanket, but it lay at her feet, sodden with Stoke's blood. Stoke kept his hurt hand on his knee, wound upward, to give it air. Bird tried to rest her mind in the creaking cart and the thuds of Apples' hooves, sounds that meant they would soon be home.

Stoke broke the silence. "It was my father I saw marked. It's my only memory of him. We were watching a parade. I was sitting on his shoulders. Rendarren came by on his war horse, and everyone was supposed to bow. My father didn't. Some Searchers saw him and marked him. I stayed on his shoulders through the whole thing, hanging on to his hair. I cried, but my father didn't cry at all. Not like me today. He would have been embarrassed, the way I hollered."

"You only screamed once," said Bird. "You don't need to feel bad about that. I won't tell anyone."

"My parents gave me to Farwender, so I could be raised in freedom and safety. Rendarren killed them shortly after that, but Farwender didn't tell me they were dead until last year."

Bird wanted somehow to comfort Stoke, to make up for all the bad things that had happened. She blurted out, "You were right. I was the one who put the ants in your bed and all the other stuff. I won't do it anymore."

Stoke smiled at her. He hardly ever smiled, so it felt especially good to Bird to see it. "Don't worry about it," he said. "Let's be friends and more than friends. Let me be a brother to you." He placed his unhurt hand over Bird's hands, which held the reins. Bird felt a flush of sweetness. "Let me be a sister to you," she answered, suddenly too shy to meet his eyes. But then she thought of Twist and Piper. They would never be her friends again.

They arrived home at dusk. Issie and Dren spilled from the cottage, calling, "They're here, they're here," with Ally galumphing behind them, his lion's head *grrring*, his snake tail making curlicues and flickering its tongue. Then came Soladin, with a dishcloth over her shoulder. Finder stayed on the porch, her fluffy white tail circled neatly about her feet. She never liked to seem too eager.

Soladin immediately spied Stoke's hand, and ordered him into the cottage, calling Dren and Issie to help. Bird tended to Apples and unloading. When she came to the basket she had prepared for Twist and Piper, she wanted to put the scarves out of her sight, but it seemed wrong to throw them away, so she stuffed them into a tree hollow near the cottage. Maybe a squirrel could use the wool for a nest.

When Bird entered the cottage, Ally immediately came to her, making a soft growl-cry that told Bird of his worry and love. She knotted both her hands in his mane.

Issie was peeling potatoes and Dren was chopping cabbage. Stoke was soaking his hand in a hot herb bath that smelled of marigolds and rotten meat. He was telling Soladin and the others what had happened and had come to the part about Piper. Bird thought how Piper would have nothing to soak her hand in.

"Will Piper be all right, without doctoring?" she asked Soladin.

Soladin ripped some cloth strips for a bandage. "The black grease they smear in the wound is painful, but it kills infection. She will survive."

"Do you think we could maybe go back to Graynok, to doctor her?" asked Bird.

Soladin gave Bird a hard look. "From what Stoke has just told me, I doubt Twist would allow our help, even if Piper were dying." Soladin dried Stoke's hand and wrapped it, weaving cloth strips crisscross through his fingers and over his palm. "I blame myself for this. I should never have let you go. How could I have been so foolish."

"There's never been Searchers in Graynok before," said Bird. "How could you have known?"

"I know Rendarren." Soladin's lovely face looked old and pale. "I know better than to let down my guard against him. I had thought the Holder kept watch over us, protecting us from Rendarren's wrath. I thought many things to fool myself into thinking we were safe. But I was wrong. Surely the Holder has abandoned us. Now I know why Farwender has not returned. He is dead or worse."

Bird's father-yearning, which had not bothered her for many weeks, slammed against her heart. Her knees went wobbly and she sat down. Stoke noticed. "What is it?"

She couldn't tell him. She shook her head and waited for the feeling to pass.

Issie dumped an apronful of carrot rounds into the stew pot. "Maybe Farwender is just fine. Maybe something nice happened. Maybe he met an old friend, and they're visiting. You know how Farwender loves to talk."

"Hush, Isogolde." Soladin tied off Stoke's bandage. "I find your hopeful fantasies most irritating." Soladin held up the bloody rag that was Bird's star blanket. "I doubt this will ever come clean again. I should throw it away."

"No," Bird cried, running toward Soladin to save her greatest treasure. Soladin gave Bird a sorrowing glance and then dropped the blanket in a pail of cold water to soak.

For dinner, they had cabbage soup, and the nut cookies

from Twist and Piper's basket. They ate in silence so as not to disturb Soladin's gloomy imaginings. From that time on, Soladin ceased all mention of Farwender.

AFTER everyone was asleep, Bird stood at her bedroom window, with Ally beside her and Finder in her arms. She listened to the night sounds: tree creaks and river hush. She wanted to run away to Farwender, to help him if she could.

But she couldn't get free of Farwender's command: "You are not, for any reason, to follow me. Please honor our friendship by respecting my wishes." These words were a wall about her, keeping her at Soladin's. And more than that, she couldn't shake the feeling that if she disobeyed Farwender, something so awful that she couldn't even imagine it might happen, not just to her personally, but somehow to her friends.

The moonlight scribbled silver on the river. Bird nuzzled her face into Ally's mane and tried to hope that Farwender was that moment traveling toward her, walking the curves of the barren hills, almost home. She tried to hope her father was with him.

8

Soladin's Secret

Wrapped in light leaves of the life Tree,
Wreathèd by the wings of sparrows,
Beauty's Wen child bares the bright Seed,
Small one come in kindness plants it.
Where the Treekeep tends and deep digs,
Where the sea kind cry from scarp-sky,
Where the olden stone kings still weep,
There the Holder spends His splendor.

—PROPHECY OF THE TREE THAT SPEAKS,

PASSED DOWN BY ORAL TRADITION

NEXT afternoon in the river forest, Stoke started a game of chase with all the children and Ally and Finder. They ran farther and farther from the cottage until they reached a shady glen, where the trees and their branches formed a natural house with a high leafy roof. Exhausted and hot, the children flung themselves upon the cool damp grass and rested, lulled by the sounds of a creek nearby, and a lark farther off. Ally, as always, kept watch in all directions with his lion's eyes and snake's eyes. Finder napped at Ally's side. Bird and Issie picked tiny pink and white daisies and began to make daisy-chain garlands for their heads. Dren practiced wiggling his ears. He couldn't do it yet, but it made Bird and Issie laugh to watch him try, especially since his ears stuck out so far.

Stoke sat cross-legged, staring at his bandaged hand, seeming far off in his thoughts. After a time he said, "Issie, Dren, I've taken Bird as my sister, and she has taken me as her brother, even as you are my sister, Issie, and you are my brother, Dren. She is one of us now, and I think we should tell her everything."

Dren grinned at Bird. "No more sand in Stoke's food?" Bird was surprised to hear that Dren knew of her secret tricks.

"That's all in the past, right, Bird?" said Stoke.

"I guess," said Bird with a stab of regret.

"But would Farwender want us to tell her?" asked Issie, her eyes wide, as usual.

Bird kept silent and still, afraid any move on her part, even breathing too loudly, might shut down the conversation.

"I'm sure he would approve," said Stoke. "He should be back by now anyway. You know, we have to face the facts; Soladin may be right. He might not be coming back, and then of course he would want us to tell Bird."

"But what about Soladin? Shouldn't she be the one to tell?" said Issie.

"Soladin is already too upset about Farwender. She will just get more upset if we ask her," said Stoke.

"All right," said Dren. "Let's tell her."

"Yes," said Issie. "But Bird, I think I should warn you that this is a very sad and ugly story."

Stoke turned his intense eyes on Bird. "Do you promise not to tell these secrets no matter what on the pain of torture or death?"

"Sure," said Bird.

"What do you know about the thalasse?" asked Stoke.

Bird said, "I know it heals people and stuff. I know it's almost gone. I know it comes from a tree that is dead."

Issie interrupted, "Stoke's the only one of us that's had it. At least Dren and I don't remember having it—do we, Dren?—and I think we would. But maybe it happened and we forgot. Dren doesn't remember anything until he came to Soladin's, except for his mother lying in her rose garden covered with blood and—"

Dren interrupted, "I don't want to talk about that, Issie."

Issie tickled her chin with a daisy. "It's all Soladin's fault. She was the Treekeeper. She was supposed to guard the Tree."

Bird stopped working on her daisy chain. "Soladin did something wrong?" Soladin was so beautiful. She was so careful about keeping the rules.

"It is said that Soladin's deed was the worst ever done in Wen," said Stoke. He continued as if reciting a lesson: "The Tree grew in the Hidden Garden. You could find it only by looking through a curlicue of gold called the Key That Sees. Soladin was the Treekeeper, which meant she wore the Key on a chain around her neck. It was a great and sacred honor. But she fell in love with Rendarren. When he asked for the Key, she gave it to him."

"Rendarren? The lord of the north? Who kills all he sees?" said Bird. "Soladin loved him?"

Dren said, "Rendarren tricked her. He could trick you too, if he got the chance."

"No he couldn't," said Bird quickly.

"Rendarren is Farwender's brother," Issie cut in. "Soladin

had promised to marry Farwender, but she fell in love with Rendarren, because he's so handsome, much handsomer than Farwender. Farwender used to be the Watchman of Wen, which is like being a king. But now Rendarren has taken over his position."

Stoke picked at the bandage on his hand. "Rendarren is a very evil man. He went into the garden and chopped the Tree down."

"How could Rendarren be Farwender's brother?" asked Bird. "Farwender is so good, and Rendarren murders people."

"Farwender is a mightier warrior than Rendarren," said Stoke. "Once he fought Rendarren and would have killed him, but Soladin begged him not to."

Bird scowled at Stoke. "Just a minute. Soladin is the most perfect person I ever met. How could she have done what you say?"

Stoke sat up straighter. "Farwender told us the story. He never lies."

Issie opened her round eyes wider. "Soladin is very, very sorry about everything. That's why she gets so strange, like she is right now."

"Farwender and Soladin ran away because Rendarren wanted to kill them," said Dren. "Rendarren's been hunting them ever since. That's why they came to this barren, ugly place, where nobody knows who they are."

"Rendarren wants to destroy the Seed," said Issie.

"Right," said Stoke.

"What are you talking about?" asked Bird.

"There's a Seed to grow another Tree," said Stoke. "It's in a Locket. The trouble is, no one can open the Locket. That's one of the things Farwender and the elders are trying to figure out."

Issie finished a little daisy chain and put it on Finder's head. The cat shook it off. "The prophecies say a beautiful child will open the Locket. Farwender says that could mean beautiful on the inside or the outside or both."

"The Opener Child is supposed to be kind and helpful to others," said Dren. "But that's just something grownups say to make children behave."

"The strangest part of the prophecy is where it says the Opener will come wrapped in the leaves of the Tree and sparrow's wings," said Stoke. "Farwender says he has no idea what that means."

"Stoke thinks it's him," said Dren.

"I do not," said Stoke. He picked a grass stem and chewed it. "Anyway, I've tried to open the Locket several times and it's still shut, so it's probably not me."

"Maybe it's me," said Bird.

Issie said, "I don't mean to hurt your feelings, Bird, but I haven't noticed you being especially kind and helpful."

"Where is the Locket?" asked Bird, in case she decided to try to open it without anyone watching. And probably wherever the Locket was, Soladin's treasure was too.

"I think Farwender has it," said Stoke.

"No he doesn't," said Dren. The others looked at him in surprise.

"How do you know?" asked Issie.

"I found it last week, when Soladin made me stay in her room for putting that fat green worm in her soup." Everybody laughed, thinking of Soladin's yelp when she saw the worm on her spoon.

"So where is it?" asked Issie eagerly. All the children leaned closer to Dren.

"I found a secret cubbyhole in the headboard of Soladin's bed," said Dren. "You open it by turning a carved flower. The Locket's in there."

Bird said, "There are hundreds of carved flowers on Soladin's bed. Which is it?"

"The first daisy on the left side, next to a mouse," said Dren. "Are you going to try to open it?"

"Nope."

"You are too," said Dren. He scrunched his lips.

Bird decided to change the subject. "All right. Suppose someone opens the Locket. Then what?"

"The Seed must be planted in the Hidden Garden, where the Tree grew before," said Stoke.

"How can anyone find it? You said Rendarren has the Key That Sees."

"Yes, but we have a chimera," said Stoke. "Chimeras used to live in the Hidden Garden. They ate the fruit of the Tree. Farwender says that's why Ally loves honey, because the fruit of the Tree tasted like honey. Anyway, Rendarren thought he killed all the chimeras. He boasted about it, but somehow Ally escaped and found Soladin and Farwender. Farwender figures Ally will know how to get back to the garden, since he came from there."

Ally heard his name, and his snake tail skittered in the grass, hissing softly.

Right then, Soladin's gong called them to lunch. The children and the animals ran for home. When Bird saw Soladin waiting for them at the door, it made her feel funny, thinking of the terrible thing Soladin had done. No wonder she was so sad and strange sometimes.

In the days that followed, Bird watched for a time when she could be sure of being alone in Soladin's room, to open the secret cubbyhole. Her chance came three days later, when they were picking blackberries and Soladin sent her back to the cottage for more baskets. Bird ran all the way, rushed into Soladin's room, and twisted the daisy near the mouse. A little door swung open at once.

Inside was a small, plain wooden box. She lifted the lid. No gold, no Locket, only small scraps of parchment, all covered with Soladin's tiny, perfect handwriting. She picked up the top one and read, "This too I add to all the evil that has come from my life, that a brave boy and a little girl have had their hands painfully mutilated."

Soladin's quick, light steps sounded on the porch outside the kitchen. Hastily, Bird returned the box to the cubbyhole and shut the little door. She slipped into the larder, where Soladin found her gathering baskets. Bird never returned to the cubbyhole. She didn't want to know any more of Soladin's bitter secrets.

9

Farwender Comes Back

Then Farwender returned. He sat on the edge of my bed holding a small brown bowl. "Thalasse, little sister," he said gently. "Allow the touch of the Holder. Begin to heal."

I sat stone still. Farwender continued, "I know you are frightened. I am too. I have failed as much as you, yet see?" He marked his own forehead with the shining oil. He dipped his finger again. I saw the oil shine on his fingertip, breathed a garden smell of green and quiet. A great longing rose within me, to feel again the Holder's love. But horror rose within as well, and with strength I thought had vanished, I pushed Farwender from me. The bowl of thalasse shattered on the floor.

—*CONFESSIONS,* BY SOLADIN LEAFSTAR, TREEKEEPER OF WEN

THE leaves of the river cottonwoods turned bright yellow and twirled to earth. Every morning, when the children walked to the garden to work, their feet crunched iced grass and their toes froze. Night came before dinner now, and they ate by lamplight.

Bird noticed that Soladin worked harder than ever, canning the end of the harvest vegetables, hanging bunches of herbs to dry, wiping, washing, scrubbing. She never seemed to sleep. Sometimes she allowed the children to stay up with her, far past their bedtimes. She seemed to want their company.

The first winter storm came, rain carried on cold, gusting winds. They spent the day indoors, making blackberry jam. When night came, they barely stopped for dinner, but worked on as if, Bird thought, Soladin didn't have a pantry already bursting with jam. Outside, the wind hooted and rain clattered against the windows. Inside, the steamy kitchen smelled fruity sweet, and everything and everybody was sticky.

They had just begun the last batch of jam when, with a sudden blast of cold wet night, the door flew open. It was Farwender.

"Anybody home?" he boomed, and laughed and quickly shut the door. He wore a long thick cloak and a wide-brimmed hat, and was sopping wet, ragged, and tired-looking. He was alone.

Bird ran with the other children to greet him, but Farwender walked past them, showering them with raindrops, and went to where Soladin stood by the hearth staring at him, the purple jam spoon still in her hand, tears rivering down her cheeks.

He removed his hat and knelt. He took Soladin's hand, jam spoon and all, and kissed it. "Milady Soladin, forgive my long returning."

"Farwender," said Soladin, in a tiny voice that squeaked. Farwender rose to his feet, and then the two of them looked at each other while all the children danced around them singing, "Farwender! Farwender!" and Ally roared and pranced and Finder leaped onto Farwender's shoulder and licked raindrops from his face. But even while Bird laughed and danced, her heart was heavy with her longing for a father. Did Farwender have news about her star blanket? Was her father coming later?

Soladin said, "You must be hungry."

Farwender said, "Aye, ravenous." And then he looked at Bird and seemed to see her wretchedness. He led her to a corner away from the others and crouched down to her size. "I wasn't able to learn anything about your family or your blanket, I'm afraid. There weren't many opportunities for investigation. We must keep hope and keep searching."

Bird saw sorrow for her in Farwender's dark eyes. She turned away and wrinkled up her face and spit to keep from crying, but tears popped out of her eyes anyway. Farwender hugged her. His cloak was cold and wet and he smelled like a storm.

Farwender took off his outer garments and sat down at the table. Soladin served up bread, butter, and the new jam. Bird sidled onto the bench next to Farwender, pushing in front of Issie. Ally shoved his head into Farwender's lap to remind Farwender to pet him. But Stoke easily won the contest for Farwender's attention when he held out his palm with its vivid red scar and told his story. Bird interrupted to tell of Stoke's bravery, and how Piper had been marked, and how Twist hated her now. As Farwender listened, his face grew ever more tired and grim. "So now he's marking the hands of children. But I see such courage on your face, Stoke. You remind me of your father. They can mark your hand, but never your heart."

"I want to fight him," said Stoke.

"Me too," chorused Bird and the others.

"If Rendarren knew he had such foes, he would throw his sword into the sea," said Farwender.

"If Rendarren knew, he would have the children torn apart by dogs as after-dinner amusement," said Soladin. She went to the sink and began to scrub the jam pots.

Farwender told them the latest news, a sobering tale. His normal route through the Pokadoon Mountains had been blocked by Rendarren's soldiers. He had been forced to travel cross-country and had gotten lost in the mountains, causing his late homecoming. "More and more of Rendarren's soldiers have received the touch of the Dark Tongue," he said.

Bird startled at the mention of a dark tongue. "What's that?"

"Don't tell her. She'll have more nightmares. I'll have to get up in the middle of the night to comfort her," Soladin snapped. Bird had been having nightmares ever since the Searchers tested her. Evil things chased her, trying to make her one of them. Sometimes there was a big mouth with a dark tongue that tried to lick her. She would wake up screaming. Soladin always came to hold her.

Farwender bowed his head. "Being handled by the Searchers is no light matter, Soladin. Surely Bird deserves an explanation." He looked around at the children. "How much does Bird know already?"

There was a moment of silence. Then Stoke said quickly, "We told Bird some history, and about the Locket."

"Well and good. Now let's see," said Farwender, slipping into his storytelling voice. Bird and the other children leaned forward on their elbows to listen.

"In the time of the beginning, before the trees grew tall in the Great Forest of Wen, before the Analari walked among the children of the Holder—"

"Analari?" Bird interrupted. "Are they real?"

"Of course," said Farwender. "It's just that nobody has seen one for a bit."

"Do they eat people?"

"Never. They're the messengers of the Holder, the helpers of Wen."

"Nobody has seen an Analari since the fall of the Tree," said Soladin.

Farwender looked uneasily at Soladin, then continued. "In the time of the beginning, the Holder spoke the words that made everything that is. The Holder's words fixed the paths of the stars and the edges of the oceans and put truth and courage in the hearts of His children. We know His words again in the thalasse."

Farwender took an enormous bite of bread and jam. "But the Holder has an enemy, the Brog, a dark spirit who ever rides the wind of pride, whispering lies into folk's hearts. The Brog has come to many in a vision or a dream, offering them great power if they will only serve him. The Brog appeared to me twice, and to Soladin once, as well as to many others.

"As a young man, my brother Rendarren listened to the Brog and agreed to serve him in return for a gift, the Dark Tongue. By the Dark Tongue, Rendarren speaks lies in such a clever, tender way that folk cannot help but believe him. The Brog intends to use Rendarren to strip from the world all knowledge of the Holder and the thalasse."

Farwender licked the jam off his fingers. "By the Dark Tongue, Rendarren deceived Soladin, cut down the Tree, slew the chimeras, and conquered most of the world. It is said that the Brog himself now lives in Rendarren's tongue.

"Rendarren passes on his power to special favorites, in a ritual where it is said he licks their foreheads. These are the Searchers, who have driven some to madness."

Suddenly the night seemed darker and the storm winds howled like folk about to die by fire. Bird wished that Farwender had listened to Soladin and not spoken of these things. "But what can we do against such power?" she cried.

Farwender looked at Bird as if to pour his strength into her. "In times past, we had the thalasse, which fortified our hearts against the Brog and his schemes. But we are not hopeless even now. If the Searchers test you again, refuse to be afraid. Tell yourself a joke. Think of something simple and sweet—a daisy, or a mouse, or a friend's face. Cling to what you know is noble and good. The Searchers have no power over you, if you only resist."

As Farwender spoke, Bird searched his face for signs of fear, and saw instead the power of one who has battled great darkness and won. All at once, her fears dropped away, and she knew again the summery sweetness of the blackberry jam, the warmth of her adopted family, and the joy of Farwender home again.

"And so," said Soladin, in a sharp bitter voice, "tell us of the council. Was it worth the risk of your life?"

"And more," said Farwender. He took a deep breath. "When I anointed everyone with thalasse, the Third Sender received a vision, the first among us since the Tree's end. Really, Soladin, this is the best blackberry jam I have ever

tasted in my life." He spooned the warm runny jam on yet another slab of bread. As he lifted the bread to his mouth, the
jam dripped onto the table in big purple plops.

"Was the vision genuine?" asked Dren.

"I think so. The Third Sender is only a few years older than
you, Dren. It was his first year on the council. The vision told
us the Seed soon will be planted. We need to prepare."

"I wish I would have a vision," said Dren.

"Prepare for what?" asked Bird.

"Does that mean someone will open the Locket?" asked
Stoke. "Maybe we should get it out and try?"

"I've told you all I know," said Farwender. "It's encouraging
but mysterious."

"That was a long and dangerous trip for a bit of mysterious
encouragement," Soladin said, scrubbing the jam pots harder.

"Now, Soladin, I am safe as ever," said Farwender. "I had the
best time seeing everybody."

"How many others are left?" asked Soladin. "Are people still
deserting to Rendarren?"

"What we have lost in numbers we have gained in spirit."

"I see," said Soladin.

"So what about the Locket?" said Stoke again. "Could we
get it out?"

"Please, Stoke," said Soladin. "Surely we have tinkered
with that Locket enough already. Leave it alone."

"Could we just get it out and look at it? Please?" asked Bird.
"The others told me all about it, but I've never seen it."

"You haven't?" said Farwender. "Soladin, could we bring the
Locket out for a viewing? With nobody trying to open it?"

"Another time," said Soladin. The old sad shadows were heavy on her face. She took a wet rag and wiped up all the jam where Farwender had been eating. "Really, Farwender, try to keep your jam on your bread. You are making a horrible mess."

Bird saw that the subject of the Locket was closed. Farwender told funny stories about his adventures, but Soladin remained deadly silent and that ruined everything.

10

BIRD'S GIFT

Farwender came to the forest altar at dawn, and was lighting a candle when he heard Soladin's light, quick step. He looked up to see her cloaked and hooded in white, carrying an armload of meadow daisies.

—*A HISTORY OF WEN,* BY ISOGOLDE OF GILLADOOR

EARLY next morning, Farwender took the children mushroom-hunting so they could make a plan for cheering up Soladin. Her birthday was in ten days, and he thought they should have a surprise party. "We'll have it at my house, so we can cook and decorate without her knowing a thing about it," he said. Soladin never visited Farwender. Her tidy nature couldn't bear his messy hut. Farwender continued, "You can help me clean my house. That would really surprise her."

The children all groaned, but agreed to help. Farwender's hut was small, just big enough to squeeze in a fireplace, a bed, and a table with some stools and chairs. Most of the floor and furniture were covered with stacks of things that Farwender intended to fix, or was saving for a friend, or thought he might be needing someday. But to everyone's relief, cleaning Farwender's hut turned out to be easier than anyone had imagined. They just jammed everything into the closet and, with much leaning and heaving, shut the door.

Soladin no longer seemed to need cheering up, however. After the rocky first night of Farwender's return, she seemed happier than Bird had ever known her to be. She hummed and laughed at the least thing, as if she had a secret of her own. It was strange, but Bird didn't wonder much about it because she was hiding in her room whenever possible, busily knitting Soladin a present—bright green socks with a daisy on each toe. Green was Bird's favorite color, and Farwender had told her that daisies were Soladin's favorite flower.

On the morning of the party, Bird and the other orphans went to Farwender's to prepare the birthday feast. Farwender was an excellent cook as long as someone reminded him to stir. They fixed a big chicken stew with carrots and potatoes, and a chocolate cake with lots of chocolate frosting. It was well known that Soladin loved chocolate beyond all other flavors. Bird and Issie loved chocolate as well, and while the others were decorating and setting the table, they helped themselves to a bit of cake, from the bottom edge, where they hoped the hole wouldn't be noticed. Farwender's sharp eyes discovered the hole right away. He gave the girls a reproachful look, but then he grinned, snitched a bit of cake for himself, and plastered up the hole with gobs of frosting.

They waited until nightfall for the party. Farwender insisted they blindfold Soladin to add to the mystery, although Stoke argued the blindfold was silly because Farwender always gave Soladin a surprise birthday party, so she knew exactly what was happening. They spun Soladin around so she lost her sense of direction, and then led her to Farwender's hut, everybody laughing.

Soladin was enchanted when they took off the blindfold,

for everything was decorated with mossy twigs and dried red roses, with a centerpiece of nuts, apples, and mushrooms. Soladin's chair had been particularly heavily decorated, with rose hips and ivy vines wound around it and everything tied with lots of brightly colored yarn. About a dozen candles lit Farwender's hut in a dreamy, glowing way that Bird thought was perfect.

After everyone, including Finder and Ally, was stuffed with stew and cake, Soladin's presents were brought from hiding and stacked before her on the feasting table. Bird was excited and nervous. The green socks were beautiful, but were they big enough? What if Soladin immediately saw the little hole where Bird had dropped a stitch?

Soladin was delighted with Stoke's gift, a box of shingles and a promise to mend the roof. She oohed for several minutes over Dren's painting of the Great Forest of Wen, based on Farwender's descriptions. Bird loved the painting too, and wished she could see the Great Forest. Issie's gift was an arrangement of dried grasses and flowers. Soladin marveled over it, even though it was already falling apart, dribbling grass seed and dead petals all over the place. She gave Issie a big hug.

Farwender gave Soladin a little plant with frilly gray leaves, which he promised would have blue flowers bright as flames, come spring. He had happened upon the plant while he was lost in the Pokadoon Mountains. Soladin declared she had never seen a plant so beautiful. Last of all, Soladin opened Bird's socks. She put them on and wiggled her toes. They fit! "My feet have never felt cozier," she proclaimed as she hugged Bird. "Who told you daisies are my favorite flower?"

Then Soladin flung her arms wide as if to hug them all at once and said, "Thank you, everyone. This is the best birthday ever. And now for something to make it even better!" With that, Soladin removed a chain that had been hanging around her neck, hidden under her tunic, and held it out for everyone to see.

A flat silver oval lay on her palm, its front engraved with a gnarled tree. Bird knew at once it was the Locket, and at first she felt a bit disappointed. It was so plain. It didn't have a single diamond or ruby on it. Then she realized Soladin was holding the Locket out to her, saying, "Bird, let's see if you can open this."

Filled with wonder, Bird took the Locket from Soladin's outstretched hand. It felt warm, as if a small fire burned within. On the side was a latch as thin as a butterfly feeler. Bird knew she held something ancient, secret and promising, and suddenly she felt small and stupid. Everyone fell silent. Bird looked up at Soladin.

"Touch the latch," said Soladin. "On the side."

Holding her breath, Bird touched the latch with her fingertip. To her amazement, the Locket opened in her hand as easily as a storybook. Inside, on a cushion of bright moss, lay a tiny glass vial, from which poured a thin stream of something that seemed to be water and light at the same time. The waterlight spilled over Bird's fingers and down to the floor, where it made a glimmering pool. Ally began a lovely low purring. "Quick!" said Bird. "Get a bowl! The thalasse is running all over the floor."

Soladin knelt by Bird's chair and put her hand under Bird's hand that held the Locket. "That's not thalasse, it's just the light the Seed gives off. You can't save it. It's like a sunset. Enjoy it while it lasts. See, it's already fading." And sure enough, the spilling light dwindled, until just a glint remained in the glass vial, where the Seed must be.

"May I hold it, please?" asked Stoke.

"Me too," said Issie and Dren.

Solemnly, Bird passed the Locket to Stoke, who passed it on to Issie, who passed it to Dren.

"How did you know I could open it?" Bird asked Soladin.

"That scrap of blanket you insist upon carrying around. The day after Farwender came back, I was scrubbing his journey clothes clean. The washing put me to mind of your star blanket, and how I couldn't quite get all of Stoke's blood out of it. I thought again about the embroidery. How it's obviously Wenish. How it always feels oddly familiar. And then it came to me: 'Wrapped in light leaves of the life Tree, Wreathèd by the wings of sparrows'—that's the old prophecy. But who would have ever thought it meant a swaddling blanket embroidered with leaves and birds? And what a wonder that you would end up in my cottage with the blanket, and that I would at last overcome my burdensome self-pity enough to see your blanket for what it is."

Bird spread her star blanket on the table and examined it. "But there aren't any leaves."

"The Tree That Speaks has star-shaped leaves as big as dinner plates," said Soladin. "The stars on your blanket are leaves."

"But did my mother know I was supposed to open the Locket? Did she make the blanket thinking about that?"

"Probably not," said Farwender. "She embroidered something beautiful to keep you warm, but the Holder guided her hand without her knowing, as may happen when you make a gift of love."

Bird was holding the Locket again, treasuring the weight of it in her hand. "Can I wear it?" If she could wear it, she would feel as magnificent as a warrior queen.

Farwender leaned forward on his elbows. He wrapped one hand within the other, a fist within a fist. His eyes held a glitter of pity, which Bird did not understand until much later. "You are the Opener. The Holder has chosen you to bear the Seed to the garden, so that the Tree That Speaks may grow again. If you accept this task, you may wear the Locket."

"Sure. I accept," she said.

Farwender's voice grew stern. "Hear all I have to say before you choose! Think! This is not some trinket you have stolen from a vegetable monger. Everything depends upon the Locket."

Bird scowled up at him. "I know."

"You don't begin to know. All the powers against us are looking for this Locket. The Searchers, Rendarren, Rendarren's soldiers, the Brog himself."

She nodded, sobered by the mention of the inhabitants of her nightmares.

Farwender continued. "I don't mean you have to be afraid. The Locket will protect you. It possesses great power. Anyone who tries to take it from you, or end your life, will die."

Instantly, Bird imagined herself on horseback, in a great battle, wearing the Locket. A huge Searcher came galloping at her, sword high. He swiped at her neck to kill her and fell off his horse, dead. His dead face looked astonished.

Soladin still knelt at Bird's side. "Mostly, your task is not to give the Locket away."

"Why would I do that?"

Soladin's eyes were fastened on the Locket in Bird's hand. "The enemy could try to buy the Locket from you. Or have you thrown into a frozen, lightless dungeon until you give it up. Or fool you into thinking its side is right and ours is wrong. Or a million other dark things. Your task is a quiet one of will and self-discipline, not a noisy one of muscle and battle. It is a matter of trueness of heart."

Bird looked around the table at the faces of her friends, soft and golden in the candlelight. The joy of being chosen sang in her blood. She wanted to help. She wanted her friends to be proud of her. She wanted to be a hero. She wanted there to be thalasse in the world again, so the sick could be well, and the fearful have courage, and so at last she could know the name of her father.

"I'll do it," she said.

Farwender rose. He took the Locket from Bird, spread its thin silver chain into a circle, and slipped it over her head. "May you bear the Seed in peace," he said.

Soladin took both of Bird's hands in her own. "Be wiser than I was," she whispered.

All at once, Farwender jumped to his feet, raised his bushy eyebrows, and cried wildly, loudly, "Milady Soladin! Oh Soladin!" He picked Soladin up under her arms and, roaring with laughter, twirled her around and around while Soladin giggled and cried, "The furniture—be careful, put me down," but Farwender did not stop until he was totally dizzy. Then they both staggered around and laughed. Somehow, nothing in the tiny hut was broken by Farwender's antics. Bird and the other orphans watched dumbfounded.

"You don't have to go crazy just because Bird opened the Locket," said Stoke.

Breathing hard, Farwender answered, "Ah, Stoke, forgive us a bit of madness after all our sorrow." He lifted his arms so high his fingers touched the ceiling. "Do you realize, children? The time has come to plant the Seed!"

Everybody cheered.

But even as they cheered, Bird noticed the old sadness creep over Soladin's face again. Farwender noticed too, for nothing concerning Soladin long escaped his eye.

"What ails thee now, milady?" asked Farwender.

Soladin answered softly, "We have the Seed, but can we ever find the garden? Rendarren has the Key That Sees. He has thrown it into the deepest sea, for all we know."

"But Soladin! We've discussed this again and again. Ally will lead us. That's why the Holder sent him. Throw off your gloom—we're off to Wen." As Farwender spoke, Ally's snake tail wrapped itself around Soladin's waist. Soladin pursed her lips and folded her arms across her chest, but she stopped complaining. Farwender turned to the children. "Time to plan our journey. Let's make a list!"

Farwender loved making lists. They were always long, and he usually lost them. He grabbed a sheet of paper and an ink bottle from the mantel. "Does anyone have a feather pen?" They all felt their pockets. Nobody had a pen. Farwender opened drawers and cupboards and boxes, hunting for one.

The children and Soladin joined the search, peering under chairs, checking windowsills and desk cubbyholes. Farwender lifted up a corner of the rug. There was a big pile of dirt, but no pen.

Finally, after they had looked everywhere twice and some places thrice without success, Farwender said, "There's no hope for it. We shall have to open the closet."

All of the children gasped. Soladin looked perplexed. Farwender took the door latch firmly in his hand and opened the door.

Everything avalanched out. Scrolls and a sword and balls of yarn. Old clothes and a shovel and a haversack. Boots and spoons and buckets. Ribbons and pinecones and a hammer.

"Really, Farwender," said Soladin, in dismay. And then they all laughed, even Soladin. For there, on the very top of the pile, like a freckle on top of a nose, was a feather pen.

"Aha!" said Farwender. He seized the pen and began the list.

11

The Searchers Return

*Then I knew what I had tried so hard all afternoon not to know:
Rendarren was the enemy. I was a fool. I had betrayed the
Holder and my people. I wanted to die. I rose, gathered rocks,
put them in my pockets, and walked into the surf. A low wave
knocked me down. I rose again, fell again, and losing even the
energy to carry out my wish to drown, I sat in the wave wash
shallows, staring out to sea, wishing and wanting the hours back
that I might have the Key, that the Tree might live.*

—*CONFESSIONS,* BY SOLADIN LEAFSTAR, TREEKEEPER OF WEN

AS if in a dream, her mouth filled with laughter and singing,
Bird walked through the dry grass, scarcely noticing that
prickles were collecting on her leggings. It had been two days
since she had first opened the Locket, and still she was filled
with the wonder of it. She felt chosen and beautiful, the most
special person in the world.

Now she, the other children, and Ally and Finder were driving Farwender's fourteen sheep to their new home at Farmer
Elwig's. They were traveling north past three large round hills,
following a cross-country wheel track. Farwender had sold the
sheep to Farmer Elwig yesterday in Graynok Market. The
farmer had offered a good price, as well he might. Farwender
raised the best sheep in the land, fat and woolly.

The children had begun their trek after breakfast. Now it was nearly noon, with still no sign of Farmer Elwig's house. The sheep seemed to go slower than beetles. There was no way to hurry them. But it was a beautiful day, crisp and cold, and they had brought Apples the pony with her cart, so they could return home lickety-split. At first light tomorrow, they would begin the journey to Wen, to plant the Seed.

Soladin and Farwender were packing as the children drove the sheep. Farwender had insisted all the children go, and Finder and Ally as well, to make it easier for Soladin to think. Bird drifted along with the sheep, daydreaming. She wished she could show the Locket to Twist and Piper. Surely the magical light of the Seed would convince Twist that Farwender was a good, powerful man. Then maybe Twist and Piper would come with them to Wen. And more than ever, Bird wished she could find her father. He would be so proud of her.

Farmer Elwig turned out to be a scrawny man with a wispy red beard. He fed the children lemonade and licorice, and then introduced them to his sheep, with long stories about each one.

"The fat one with the brown spot behind the left ear is Jolly Polly," he said. "I call her that because of her sense of humor. See that little smile on her face? She's always laughing. Now the one with the really long nose is Long Nose. She's the queen of the bunch, don't you know, always looking down her nose at the others. That ewe that holds her ears out stiff is Ear Wings. She looks like she could fly like an eagle, don't you think?"

Stoke said, "This is all very interesting, but Farwender is expecting us back as soon as possible."

"Have some more licorice," said Farmer Elwig. "Now over there, you have the twins, Fluffy and Puffy. Fluffy is the one with the wild look in her eye. She bites sometimes. Don't know what to do about it. I pet her extra, whisper kind words, but see this scar on my hand? Fluffy's work."

By the time the children were joggling along for home in the pony cart, it was late afternoon, and getting cold. Stoke drove the cart, while Dren, Issie, Bird, and Finder sat in the back, in a nest of sweaters and hats. Farwender had wanted them to give the sweaters and hats to Farmer Elwig, but the farmer had insisted he was warm enough already, thank you, although it was lovely knitting. Ally walked alongside Apples, switching his snake tail through the grass, hunting grasshoppers. Despite the bumpy ride, Bird and Issie were trying to knit nose warmers, for their journey would take them through the Pokadoon Mountains in winter. They would probably have to travel by dogsled. Bird was knitting Farwender a big red nose warmer, "to match his nose," she said to Issie, and they giggled.

As the sky turned dusky, they came at last to the main road. They noticed a thick plume of black smoke rising from the direction of their home.

"Soladin must have made Farwender burn all his trash," said Dren. "She must be so happy."

"But it's so much smoke," said Bird.

"Farwender has heaps of trash," said Issie.

They were approaching the canyon's edge, where a few moons ago Bird had stood in the night and seen the light that Farwender always left burning for those in need.

"Whoa!" Stoke called. "Let's take a look."

Bird dropped her knitting and stood up in the cart with the others to see. In the river canyon far below, orange flames bloomed in the dusk. The hut, cottage, and barn were all on fire.

Issie screamed. Bird would have jumped from the cart and run down the hill, but Stoke grabbed her arm. "It's the Searchers," he said. "Look." In the clearing around Soladin's cottage, Bird could make out swarms of black-robed men, mounting horses. Two of the horses had double riders. Bird clenched her fists in dismay. None of the children spoke what all knew: Farwender and Soladin had been captured.

Issie started to cry. Stoke said, "Quick! They're coming this way! Hide!" The children led Apples with her cart into a thicket of dry thorn and deerbrush, leaving a trampled path in the dry grass.

Stoke ordered, "Issie, on lookout. Tell us when they're close. Bird and Dren, help me make the grass stand up." Feverishly yet carefully, they tried to make the broken grass stand again, to cover their tracks. It was hopeless. The silver Locket swung from Bird's neck as she bent to her task. She tucked it back inside her tunic where the Searchers wouldn't see it. They can't have it, she vowed to herself. I won't let them.

In no time Issie cried, "Here they come!"

The children pushed into the thicket, Ally following. The thorns tore at their clothing and skin. Deep in the scrub, they stopped. They crouched and waited. Already Bird could faintly hear thudding hooves and jingling saddle gear. Looking through the brush, she could see the tramped grass pointing plain as a road to their hiding place. The Searchers would notice for sure. What would they do when they caught her? Fear gushed through her, pushing her heart to beat faster, faster. Maybe they should fight. If only she had a knife, or even her knitting needles. The Searchers couldn't kill her, but they could capture her and kill her friends. She crouched down farther, into a little ball. Ally was on one side of her, Stoke on the other, and now Stoke took her hand. She felt the ridges of his X scar.

Issie whispered, "Look! Finder!" There was the white cat, resting next to the road, as if the whole reason for stopping was to have a picnic.

Before anyone could stop him, Ally leaped from the thicket. In two more leaps, the chimera reached Finder, picked her up by the scruff of her neck, and then bounded back to the hiding place. Issie took Finder from Ally's mouth and held her.

The black riders appeared over the canyon brink, dozens of them, two abreast, in close formation, ghost shapes in the twilight. Farwender and Soladin each rode behind a Searcher. Their hands were tied behind their backs. Even through the brush in the twilight, Bird could see that Farwender bled from a gash on his cheek. One of the sleeves of Soladin's tunic was ripped off, and her braids had come loose from their crown and swung free. Both Soladin and Farwender looked straight ahead, their heads held high. They seemed unafraid, and Bird felt proud of them, even as her every nerve squealed with fear.

As the Searchers rode past, a few of them looked directly at the mashed grass. But then one of the Searchers spied something overhead; it seemed to be a large bird. He pointed to it, and all the other Searchers looked up and away from the hiding place. But Farwender gave the trampled grass a quick look, and Bird imagined he knew they were there.

The children waited silently in the brush until long after the hoofbeats died away. Bird and Stoke kept holding hands. Finally the orphans felt safe enough to head down into the canyon to see what was left of their home. Night had fallen, and a round moon pushed its belly up from behind the hills. The fires were still busy, finishing their work. They stayed in the cart, well back from the heat and the burning, falling timbers. The noise was deafening. Bird felt overwhelmed. How could everything be gone, just like that? At Farwender's flaming hut, Ally lifted both of his heads to the moon and hissed and yowled. Fearing that the noise might bring Searchers, Bird tried to hush him, but the chimera, usually obedient to her slightest whim, would not heed her.

Stoke said, "We'd better get out of here. What if the Searchers come back?"

They made camp downriver, some distance from the road, where they couldn't be easily seen. They reckoned a campfire would be dangerous—what if the Searchers saw it?—so they sat in the dark in the sweater nest of the pony cart. They ate in dazed silence—bread and cheese left from lunch and the last four pieces of Farmer Elwig's licorice. Apples munched grass, and Ally and Finder went hunting.

Finally Dren said, "Do you think Soladin and Farwender are still alive?"

"I'm sure they are," said Stoke. "The Searchers would have killed them on the spot unless they planned to take them to

Wen, to Rendarren. I propose we follow behind as fast as possible and do our best to rescue them."

"How can four children rescue anybody from the Searchers?" asked Dren.

"We'll find a way if we look for it," said Stoke. "The Holder will help us."

Bird wondered why the Holder hadn't protected Soladin and Farwender from getting caught in the first place, but she didn't say this. Instead she said, "At least we've been practicing our sword fighting." Farwender had started their training upon his return. They'd had only three lessons.

"And we still have the Locket," said Issie. "That's what Rendarren really wants."

"And we have lots of money," said Stoke. "Fourteen pieces of gold for the sheep."

"And we have Ally," said Bird. "He's worth a hundred Searchers in a fight."

Dren sighed. "I give up. It will be as easy as eating cake for four children to rescue two of Rendarren's most-wanted prisoners." At that, Bird threw one of Farwender's sweaters at Dren, and before they knew it, they were all flinging sweaters and laughing.

But soon they stopped and fell silent. Nobody could think of anything more to say except what they were afraid of, or how they wished there were more to eat. Bird tried to comfort herself by listening to the familiar sounds of the forest, the pouring river waters and the *ching-ching* of the crickets, but everything seemed changed, cold and hard. The night seemed impossibly large and dark, and she felt far too small. Her heart was heavy with father-wanting, and even though she held tightly to her star blanket, the weight on her chest wouldn't go away.

After a time, Issie said, "Bird, could you open the Locket?"

"Sure." Bird pulled out the Locket from under her tunic. Its silvery surface glimmered in the moonlight. It opened at her touch and poured into the night a rainbow of sparks. Bird passed the Locket around, so the others could have the comfort of holding it. In time the sparks ceased, but the Seed light burned on, a tiny twinkle.

"I think we should have a time of thanks, like we always used to," said Stoke. "I'll start. I'm thankful to the Holder that the Searchers didn't see the obvious trail that led straight to our hiding place. Maybe the Holder sent that bird in the sky, just at the right time."

"I'm thankful that Farwender and Soladin are still alive," said Dren. "At least I hope they are."

"I'm thankful that we're still alive," said Bird. "So we can rescue Soladin and Farwender."

"I'm thankful we still have the Locket, and that Bird can open it. As long as we have that, I think there is hope," said Issie.

After that, they went to sleep, with Ally in the middle of everybody for a heater and Finder snuggled between Bird and Issie. As always, Bird spread her star blanket under her head. It was freezing cold, but the children were toasty warm under Farwender's rainbow sweaters.

12

WHAT REMAINED

The thalasse gave off a silvery light, like star shine on dark
water. It smelled like a well-watered garden at dawn.

—*CONFESSIONS*, BY SOLADIN LEAFSTAR, TREEKEEPER OF WEN

THE children woke at first light, hungry. There was nothing to
eat. The sweaters covering them were stiff with frost, but they
remained warm enough underneath. Smoke from the fire hung
in the forest, soiling the morning light. A burnt stench filled
their noses. They went at once to see if anything was left of
their home.

At Soladin's cottage, everything was burned except the
chimney and the foundation wall of river rock. Stoke systematically paced the charred ground, while Dren kicked at burnt
chunks. Ally sniffed everything with both his lion's nose
and his flickering snake's tongue. Issie looked for useful ob-
jects, such as a piece of a cup or bowl big enough to clean and
use again. She discovered that all the crockery had been
smashed.

With Finder trailing behind her, Bird left the others and
walked to the ruins of Farwender's hut. There she wandered,
crunching cinders underfoot, her hunger for a father squeezing
her chest so hard that she could scarcely breathe. She held her
star blanket against her cheek, but the wanting only got worse.

She didn't only want a father. She wanted Farwender. She wanted him to say her name and make her honeybread. She wished she could find a little scrap of something that would have Farwender in it, that she could always keep in case she never saw him again.

Loud meowing from Finder broke into Bird's thoughts. She rushed to the cat's side and picked up a blackened object Finder was pushing with her nose. Even covered with soot, the distinctive crystal shape of the thalasse vial was easy to recognize. The silver stopper was gone. Bird scrubbed off the soot with some spit and raised the vial to the sun, to see if perhaps a drop or two of the shining oil somehow remained in the vessel. It was empty. So it ends, she thought, her heart sinking. How Soladin would grieve if she knew, and perhaps she does know.

Bird pocketed the vial and trudged back to the others. Issie greeted her, triumphantly waving blackened scissors, the same scissors Stoke and Bird had gotten fixed in Graynok. Ruefully, Bird pulled out the thalasse vial and shook it upside down so the others could see that it was empty. Stoke shrugged his shoulders. "That's what I was looking for too. We might as well go." His voice sounded empty.

Bird held out the vial to him. "Here. You keep it."

Bird couldn't read the thoughts that passed behind his dark eyes. He took the vial. "Thanks," he said.

Immediately she wanted the vial back, but it was too late. Then Stoke smiled at her, his rare wide grin, his whole face happy, and she was glad she had given him the vial after all.

The children left at once for Graynok. They figured if they

were going to rescue Farwender and Soladin, they had best hurry. And they could buy food in Graynok. They were all hungry, and the river forest offered little to eat. What berries remained were rotten, and the hickory nut bushes had been picked clean by squirrels.

Bird figured the Searchers must not be looking for them, otherwise some of the black-robed riders would have stayed behind to catch them. The others agreed. They decided they could safely travel by day, as long as nobody saw Stoke's hand or Ally. To Ally's dismay, the children hid him in the cart under sweaters, in case someone nosy happened along.

They took turns walking beside the cart to spare Apples, who had a heavy chimera to pull up and down the hills. It was a dusty march, but they slaked their thirst often from their water skins, filled with Rilla Nilla water, a taste of home. Apples went slowly, especially uphill, and it was late afternoon before they finally neared Graynok. Here they pulled off the main road and went overland a long way before they stopped and hid the cart in the scrub. Ally, finally allowed to crawl out from under the sweaters, refused to let anyone pet him, but went off in a huff into the grasslands.

During the journey to Graynok, Bird had thought long about Twist and Piper. She had decided to find Twist and show her the Locket. Maybe she could convince Twist and Piper to join them on their rescue mission.

Now, as the orphans sat in the dry grass discussing what they might do next, Bird suggested her idea to the others. "That's a terrible plan," said Stoke immediately, crossing his arms over his chest. "She wasn't too friendly the last time you saw her. She'd probably turn you in to the Searchers, first chance."

Dren and Issie agreed. Dren thought Bird shouldn't even go near Graynok. "The Searchers probably questioned everybody. They'll know you are Farwender's friend and they'll be looking for you."

"Then Stoke should stay behind too," said Bird. "Graynok folk have seen him with me."

Reluctantly, Stoke agreed, and Issie and Dren excitedly set out for town.

"Be fast," Bird called out after them. "Remember there are hungry people back here."

Issie and Dren returned at nightfall loaded with cheese, bread, and information. Everybody kept warm under the sweaters in the cart. Stoke and Bird ate while Issie and Dren reported. The market had been abuzz with news of the Searchers, who had spent the previous night in Graynok with two prisoners—Farwender and a golden-haired woman. According to market tittle-tattle, Farwender and the woman were dangerous criminals, intended for Rendarren's dungeons or worse. At dawn, most of the Searchers had taken the prisoners off toward the mountains, to Wen, but a handful of the black-robed riders remained in Graynok. They were offering a thousand pieces of gold for a silver Locket, of ancient work, engraved with a tree.

"I felt so scared when the baker said that," said Issie. "I felt like he could see straight into my brain and know I knew all about the Locket. He even asked me if I knew a girl named

Bird, 'a dark-eyed skinny child who bites people.' Do you bite people?"

"I used to when I was younger," said Bird.

"Is there a reward for Bird?" asked Stoke. "If she starts biting again, we can turn her in." He laughed as if this were funny.

Dren said, "Fifty gold pieces," and Stoke stopped laughing. Bird was thrilled. She was worth as much as fifty sheep.

"Is there a reward for me?" Stoke asked.

"Nope, sorry, but they want Ally—a hundred gold pieces," said Dren.

"Did you hear that, Ally? You're famous," Issie called out to the chimera, who had returned from sulking, and lay near the cart.

Dren said, "Good thing you didn't come, Stoke. They were collecting all the thalasse folk in a prison cart to take to Rendarren—everybody with an X. They're going from town to town."

"They'll catch Piper," said Bird. "I have to warn Twist."

Dren said, "Slow down, Bird-legs. It's all done and finished. The cart already left. There's nothing you can do about it."

"Did you see if they had Piper?"

"We didn't see the cart at all."

"We've got to find out what happened. I've got to see Twist right now," said Bird.

"I'll go with you," said Stoke.

"Twist will talk better if I go alone," said Bird. "Don't worry. I'm an expert at sneaking around Graynok. Besides, I've got the Locket. No one can kill me."

"But what if you get caught?" said Stoke. "What if the Searchers can sense the presence of the Locket, just like the thalasse?"

"What if the Locket doesn't work like everyone thinks?" said Dren.

Bird hated them telling her what to do. She tore off half a loaf of bread to take with her. "I'll be really fast," she said. And before anybody could stop her, she was off, trotting through the dry sticker grass into the night.

The immense orange moon gave good light and Bird easily found her way to the main road. It felt good to be doing something after waiting around in the hills all afternoon. She decided not to enter the city through the broken gates, because Searchers might be guarding there. Instead, she climbed through the wall at a wrecked place she knew. Then she slipped through the city to her old lordhouse, always staying in the shadows. As a special precaution, instead of entering the lordhouse through the front door, Bird climbed the side of the house and crawled in Twist's upstairs window. She knew the foot- and handholds in the stone wall as well as she knew the stairs.

Twist lay asleep on her straw pallet, dusted in moonlight. Piper was nowhere to be seen. Bird crouched at Twist's side and shook her shoulder. "Twist, it's me, Bird."

Twist shuddered and quickly sat up.

"Where's Piper?" Bird scanned the room, hoping she had overlooked Piper's tiny form.

"They took her," Twist said, in a harsh, low voice. "Because of the thalasse. It's your fault. Go away."

"Where did they take her?"

"I don't know. To Rendarren. To death." Twist stifled a sob. Bird reached her arm around her friend to comfort her, but Twist pulled away and hissed, "Get out. Get out or I'll scream. There's a Searcher in the house, you know, waiting for you. They know all about you."

"I'll go, I promise. But first, let me show you something."

Twist shook her head. "Get out of here. This is my last warning. For friendship's sake, I'm not screaming. I'm giving you a chance."

"For friendship's sake I'm showing you this." Bird pulled out from under her tunic the silvery Locket, engraved with the Tree That Speaks. "Isn't it beautiful? It holds some kind of ancient magic. It's more powerful than anything, even Rendarren."

"So *you* have it. Who'd you steal it from?"

"It's rightfully mine," Bird whispered to her friend. "Look!" She touched the Locket open. To Bird's amazement, fire spilled into the room, huge spiking flames, taller than she was. But the flames didn't burn anything; they didn't even feel warm.

Twist screamed.

"Hush!" said Bird. "They'll hear you." Hoping to stop Twist's screams, she shut the Locket and slipped it back under her tunic, but it was too late. Boots were clumping fast up the grand staircase. The Searcher would be there soon. Bird whispered fiercely, "Come on! Help me rescue Piper! And Farwender and Soladin too!"

"Farwender!" said Twist in a whisper that seemed like a yell.

"Who do you think told the Searchers about Farwender! I told them. I told them everything—about you, about Farwender, about that boyfriend of yours." Twist choked back another sob. "They promised they would give back Piper. But they lied."

"How could you!" said Bird.

"We're doomed," sobbed Twist. "We're all doomed."

Bird jumped to her feet. "Shut up!" she said. She felt like hitting Twist, but there wasn't time.

The heavy boots sounded in the hallway now. Twist whispered mournfully, "Quick, out the window. I'll tell them I had a bad dream."

Bird shot over the windowsill, down the side of the house, and into the shadows that she knew better than anybody. As she fled through Graynok and then the barren hills, her heart was emptier than it had ever been, thinking of Piper's capture and Twist's betrayal. When she returned to camp, she found the other children asleep. Only Ally and Finder were awake, lying together in the dry grass, keeping watch. Bird roused her friends and told them what she had learned. "The Searchers took Piper. Twist told the Searchers about me and Farwender and you too, Stoke. She said she thought it would save Piper."

"So she is our enemy," said Stoke. "I told you."

"But it's understandable, in a way," said Issie. "She only did it to save Piper. At least she helped you escape."

"I hate her," said Bird. She spit into the dry grass. "We should rescue Piper and not give her back to Twist. We should keep her with us."

"What if Twist changes her mind and tells the Searchers she's just seen you and the Locket?" asked Dren.

"We have to go. Now. As fast as we can, as far as we can," said Stoke.

They left at once, following the road into the Pokadoon Mountains. Ally refused to ride under the sweaters. Instead he strode beside the cart, his lion's head huge and shaggy in the moonlight. Bird doubted they would catch up to the Searchers who held Farwender and Soladin until they reached the land of Wen, for the Searchers rode swift horses. But there was a chance, Bird kept thinking, that they might overtake the prison cart carrying Piper. Bird hoped someone in the cart was playing silly games with Piper, helping her not to be afraid, holding her.

13

An Argument in the Snow

Soladin's fingers ceaselessly worked at the clasp of the Locket she wore around her neck. She picked and pried until her fingers bled, until the blood spattered her tunic, but it would not open.

—*A HISTORY OF WEN,* BY ISOGOLDE OF GILLADOOR

THEY slept by day and traveled by night, always in haste and fear. The hills gave way to forested steeps, and the road of dust became a road of broken rocks that bruised their feet. The moon withered and then began anew. The weather held clear, but ever colder. Soon everything would be shrouded with snow.

They wore Farwender's sweaters against the cold. Bird chose an orange sweater with blue polka dots, so large it fell below her knees. On the top of the green hood was a yellow pom-pom the size of Farwender's fist. It was that size, Bird knew, because Farwender had made the pom-pom by wrapping the yarn around his hand.

Village by village they bought provisions—fruit, meat, nuts, fur robes, packs, journey bread. They made their purchases bit by bit, not wanting to arouse suspicion by buying everything at once. They had plenty of money from having sold the sheep to Farmer Elwig. Dren and Issie did all the shopping, so Stoke and Bird wouldn't risk capture, for everywhere they went there were Searchers. Dren bargained well and made their money go far. Issie was fearless, confident that her cuteness and charm were enough to protect her, and Dren too. Bird worried that strange children were bound to provoke the wrong kind of interest, and she was relieved each time the two returned from their forays. After a few shopping trips the children had everything they needed except swords. Folk would be entirely too suspicious of children buying swords. Issie cleverly managed to take the scissors apart, creating two blades that were like small daggers, and then they bought two vegetable knives, and that had to do for weapons.

From the market gossip, Issie and Dren learned the Searchers holding Farwender and Soladin were traveling almost at a gallop, exchanging tired horses for fresh ones at outposts along the way. They were probably deep into the Pokadoon Mountains by now, headed toward Sea Rim, the capital city of Wen, where Rendarren had his dungeons. As for Piper and the others taken in the prison cart, nothing could be discovered. Stoke guessed the cart had gone the opposite direction, to the sea. The cart prisoners would be transported to Wen by ship, a much slower journey, but one that avoided winter passage through the mountains. Bird's heart sank when she heard this. She had wanted to rescue Piper first.

Everywhere folk said that anyone who tried to cross the mountains after the snows would freeze to death. And everywhere folk spoke of the Searchers' rewards for the silver Locket, the chimera, and the dark-eyed skinny girl known to bite.

As the children journeyed on each night, they were ever alert for the sound of approaching travelers, especially on horseback. The minute they heard anything—Ally always heard first, stopping and lifting both his heads—they would pull off into the bushes. One night, as they crouched behind trees below the lip of the road, a cadre of Searchers jingled by at a trot. Bird peeked and saw the gold scrollwork on their helmets glinting in the moonlight. Fortunately, the night and the forest shadows hid the children well, and the Searchers never guessed how close they came to all they sought.

In the beginning, Bird thought the Pokadoon Mountains looked like tiny white teeth on the horizon, so far away it seemed it would take a year to reach them. Then for many days, the mountains disappeared, hidden by the rising nearer hills. Finally one dawn, after a long night of travel, the children rounded a wide curve and there were the mountains again, startlingly close, impossibly steep, a wall of spires and slabs, beautiful to see, awful to think of traveling through.

"I think we'd better talk," Dren said, reining Apples to a halt before the fearsome view. "Those mountains are much bigger than I thought. The villagers might be right about folk dying up there in winter. Maybe we should wait until spring."

"Farwender and Soladin will probably be dead by spring," said Stoke matter-of-factly. "Anybody who wants can stay behind in the next village. I'm going on."

"They might be dead already," Dren muttered under his breath.

Bird, sitting beside Dren on the cart bench, gave him a dirty look. The mountains looked bigger and colder than she had imagined too, but nothing would stop her from trying to rescue her friends.

Issie was stroking Apples' nose. "Maybe we could hire a guide to help us through the mountains."

"That's a stupid idea," said Stoke. "The guide might just turn us in to Rendarren."

"Well, maybe we could get a dogsled," said Issie. They had all heard of dogsleds in Farwender's stories. "Apples could carry the sled in the cart until we come to the snow. Then we could sell Apples and the cart and have Ally pull the dogsled."

"We don't know anything about dogsleds. And Ally's not nearly as strong as a pack of dogs," said Stoke. "I vote no."

"Folk might get suspicious if they saw strange children buying a sled," said Dren. "I vote no too."

"No," said Bird.

"All right," said Issie. "But we have to think of something soon. What if it snows tonight?"

Stoke looked around as if assessing everybody's strength. "We'll just put on our packs and follow Ally the best we can."

Dren rubbed his head, making his hair poke out even more than usual. Bird wished hard that it would never, ever snow.

That morning they made camp on the bank of a creek spilling through a ferny glen, a pleasant spot, with no view of the jagged mountains. A village lay in the steep valley below. Gray puffy clouds were gathering as they went to bed, but clouds had been gathering and ungathering for days now. Bird fell asleep peaceful and warm.

She woke up suddenly into a dark gray day. Wet cold things, which she decided must be snowflakes, were dropping on her face. She had never seen snow before. The flakes, as big as daisies, were piling silently and quickly on top of everything. She woke the others and together they tied a canvas over the cart and another between some trees to shelter Apples. Then they put on their new fur robes and climbed into the cart tent. At first they couldn't help but be delighted. They were snug enough, and Apples had her blanket and shelter. They had thought of everything, and the snow was lovely. They fell back asleep.

After a time, Bird thought she heard Stoke moaning. It sounded as if he had a terrible fever. She tried to go to help, but she couldn't move. Her feet were anchored by something heavy and frozen. Then she realized she was dreaming, woke up, and discovered that a wind was howling up the mountain draw. Her feet were buried in snow that had blown under the canvas. Despite her boots and thick socks, her feet were numb.

She lifted the canvas and peered outside into a gray, swirling world. She could barely make out Apples tied to the tree next to the cart. The others woke too, all freezing. Issie's teeth chattered; she couldn't make them stop. To warm her up, Bird had her lie next to Ally, which seemed to help. Then Stoke, Dren, and Bird battened down the canvas, taking off their mittens to tie and retie knots with numb clumsy fingers. But no matter what they did, the wind blew more and more snow under the canvas, where it melted and made everything wet. Finally they gave up struggling with the canvas and bunched together around Ally. "We have to make a fire," said Stoke.

"Where will we make it?" asked Dren. "Where will we find dry wood?"

"What if this goes on for days and weeks?" said Issie through chattering teeth. "Let's go to the village. We'll die out here."

"You can't find the village in this blizzard," said Stoke. "We'll be fine right here. We've got lots of food." A gust of wind pushed a tent side against them.

"I've heard it's painless to freeze to death," said Dren.

"Stop it," said Bird. "We're not going to freeze to death. Let's eat something."

They got out the chocolate. There wasn't much left. They would have eaten all of it, but Stoke made them save some— a big bite apiece—for later, in case of emergency. The chocolate lifted their spirits, but didn't make them any warmer. Bird's whole body was shaking. She had never been so cold.

"Let's think of something warm," suggested Stoke.

"A big stew," said Bird.

"Do you always have to think of food?" said Stoke. "Soladin's bathtub."

"A hot rock by the river in the sun," said Dren.

"I don't want to be cold," Issie whined, sticking her chin up in the air like a three-year-old. "I'm too cold."

"Calm down, Issie," said Dren. "You'll be all right. You can have my coat."

"Your coat is all wet," wailed Issie. "I don't care what you say: I'm going to the village."

"I'll go with you," said Dren.

"You come with us too, Stoke," said Bird.

"Bird? You're going?" Stoke asked.

"Of course. I'm not stupid," said Bird. Everybody but Stoke got ready to go, pulling on knit hats and winding scarves around their necks and faces until just their eyes showed.

"Good luck finding the village in this blizzard," said Stoke, as Bird and the others climbed from the cart.

"Ally will find it. He can find anything. Come on, come with us," begged Bird. Outside the shelter of the cart, the storm hit full force. The wind found a way to blow down Bird's neck, freezing her more than ever. She and the others hurriedly formed a chain, holding hands, with Ally at the lead, Bird grasping Ally's tail, then Issie and Dren.

Stoke stuck his head out of the tent and yelled, "I won't go. It isn't right. I don't care if I do freeze to death. You'll all be captured. We'll never plant the Seed. Do you want Farwender, Soladin, and Piper to die?"

Bird yelled back at him, "We won't be much good to them frozen to death, will we? We have to go, right now. Come on!" As the storm howled all around them, Bird and the others waited for Stoke to say something, to change his mind, but Stoke stayed silent. So finally Bird yelled at Ally, "Village, Ally, village!"

Just about then, she felt something as heavy as a sugar sack land on her shoulder. It was Finder. From Bird's back the cat leaped onto Ally's back and from there, clinging with her claws, made her way to Ally's head, and burrowed into his mane.

As Ally led them away down the mountain, Bird heard Stoke cry above the wind, "Go ahead, take Finder, see if I care!" Bird looked back to see Stoke's face, but all she could make out in the storm gloom was the gray, ragged shadow of the cart with the wind-whipped canvas tied over it.

14

Discovered

In the confusion that followed, the people of Wen scattered in all directions, driven by fear, longing only to be as far as possible from the fallen Tree That Speaks. As they fled, some of them prayed to the Holder, imploring His help, asking why such evil had befallen them. Others reviled the Holder, vowing they would never speak His name again except to curse.

—*A HISTORY OF WEN,* BY ISOGOLDE OF GILLADOOR

ALL afternoon, Ally broke a path through the knee-deep snow, and the children stumbled after him, steeply downhill through a forest of gray ghost trees and swirling white. As Bird forced her numb feet to take step after step, she kept thinking about Stoke. Part of her yearned to go back to him, to make him see he had to come with them. But her feet kept marching forward.

After a time, they left the forest, and the way leveled out. Without the trees to soften the storm, the wind and snow became an icy white wall they had to keep pushing through, again and again. The wind-driven flakes stung Bird's eyes, so she shut them. She couldn't see where they were going anyway. She just hoped Ally had the amazing sense of direction Farwender said he had. For all she knew, Ally was leading them into the wilderness, to be frozen forever.

Then slowly, the wind became less fierce. Bird opened her

eyes to see the dark gray shapes of houses and yellow squares of window light. They passed so near one window that she saw sitting before a fire, a boy and a girl nestled on their father's lap. The father seemed to be telling his children a story.

Bird's father-wanting pressed upon her. She let go of Ally's tail. She raised her hand to knock on the window, but Dren grabbed her arm, shaking his head. He pulled the scarf down from his mouth, then put his mouth to her ear and said, "They might turn us in to the Searchers."

Woken back to her senses, Bird again gripped Ally's tail. The children and the chimera plodded on. Soon a large dark barn loomed before them. Inside there was a black cow and a haystack as big as Farwender's hut. High windows filled the barn with gray light.

They took turns squirting the cow's warm milk into their mouths. The feeling returned to their numb toes and fingers with a stinging burning that finally gave way to delicious warmth. They dug beds into the haystack, arranging themselves so the farmer wouldn't see them when he came that evening to milk the cow. Bird was worried that Ally would try to protect them from the farmer, so she had Ally lie near her, with his tail wound around her arm. If Ally moved, she would wake up. The hay was scratchy, but it smelled like summer in the dry grass hills of Graynok. Soon even Issie, with Finder cuddled close, was talking about how cozy she felt.

"I hope Stoke's all right," said Bird as she laid her head on her star blanket.

"We should have made him come with us," said Issie from her burrow nearby.

"You can't make Stoke do anything," said Dren. "Someday he's going to die of his own stubbornness—that's what Soladin always says."

It was late afternoon now, and they had been robbed of their customary daytime sleep. Warm and full, despite their worries about Stoke, all three fell deeply asleep.

BIRD woke to a sound that made her instantly alert—Ally growling low. She heard the quick *wifft* of metal upon metal, as of a sword being drawn from its scabbard. Ally's tail was no longer wrapped around her arm. Night had come, but the barn was filled with light. Immediately, silently, she crept from her hay burrow and peered around the giant haystack. A lantern had been hung on the wall. The barn door was partly open, and near it crouched Ally, ready to spring at a man who held a drawn sword. The man lunged at Ally. The chimera stepped aside and the sword pierced the haystack, not far from where Issie and Dren lay sleeping. The man jumped back, ready to attack Ally again. With a roar as loud as a waterfall, Ally leaped at the man, knocking him flat on his back. The man tried to roll away, but Ally pinned him with a front paw while his snake tail danced over the man's face, mouth wide open, fangs extended, ready to strike.

"Stop, Ally, stop!" Bird yelled, unwilling to see Ally hurt the man. With a mournful look upon his lion's face, Ally lifted his paw. The man scrambled to his feet and fled.

Bird pulled the barn door closed. Ally stayed at the door, sniffing at the cracks. Issie and Dren emerged sleepily from the haystack. "The farmer found us, but Ally chased him off," Bird told them. "We'd better get out of here. He'll be back with re-inforcements."

"Let's stay and talk to him," said Issie, finger-combing hay from Finder's fur. "He probably thought we were burglars. I'm sure he'll understand when he sees that we're children."

"He'll understand he can get a pile of gold by turning us in," said Dren.

"But where will we go? I'll freeze again," said Issie.

"We have to go back to Stoke. It's Stoke or get caught." As she said this, Bird realized she was worried about Stoke and glad to go back to him.

With Issie still pouting, the three children left the barn. "Find Stoke," Bird instructed the chimera, and off they went into the night. They went as they had come, holding hands with Ally at the lead and Finder riding on top of Ally's head. All that could be seen of Finder was her ears poking out of the thatch of Ally's mane. The snow was so deep they would have sunk to their waists with each step if Ally hadn't gone first, pushing out a ditch.

Soon they heard dogs barking somewhere behind them. Then they saw torches, far off, quickly coming closer. "Oh snot," Bird muttered to herself. "They've got a dogsled."

"Faster!" she shouted to Ally.

The villagers rapidly gained on the children, following along in the ditch Ally had made. The dogs barked louder and louder. Bird fought her way to Ally's head, pulling herself hand-over-hand along his tail, clutching fur along his back, until she got to his front. "Ally!" she yelled fiercely in his ear. "Attack!" Then she let go of him.

Obedient to his mistress' call, roaring louder than the storm, Ally left the children and bounded toward the oncoming villagers. Bird peered into the snow-clogged darkness, trying to get some idea of what was happening. The torches moved away and then disappeared. The barking stopped. Ally must have forced the villagers back, Bird reasoned. She huddled together with the others and waited for Ally to return. Hours seemed to pass. The storm swirled so wild and thick, it seemed to her they had been swallowed by a snow monster.

Finally, Bird yelled, "Ally! Ally! Ally!" even though she knew Ally probably couldn't hear her. Dren and Issie took up the cry—"Al-ly! Al-ly!" they screamed with her. The three children clung to each other, waiting and hoping that soon Ally would emerge from the dark blizzard and take them back to Stoke.

"I'm cold!" Issie shouted each word distinctly so the other two could hear her. Bird sighed with disgust. Issie was such a baby.

"Stomp your feet, swing your arms!" shouted Dren. All of them marched in place in the snow.

After a time Issie shouted, "I'm getting colder!"

Dren shouted, "Let's go! Ally's not coming back!"

Bird shouted, "We can't find Stoke without Ally!"

"I want to go!" shouted Issie.

"Two to one! Come on, Bird!" shouted Dren.

"No!" shouted Bird.

"Ally's probably dead!" shouted Dren.

Dren might be right, Bird thought. They had been waiting a long time. "He might be hurt! We have to help him!" she shouted back.

"I'm going on!" shouted Issie. She tried to run off, but Bird grabbed her and held her fast.

"Open the Locket!" Dren yelled in Bird's face.

The Locket was under two sweaters and a fur robe. "I can't!" yelled Bird.

Then, out of the stormy darkness, something large and furry pushed its way into the children's huddle. All three orphans instantly forgot their quarrel. As they hugged Ally's enormous furry head—the size of three people's heads—they heard a piercing angry meow. Underneath a tangle of snowy mane, Finder still clung to Ally's head. The white cat sounded so mad and silly that they all laughed, despite the situation.

Ally started nudging the children, first one, then another, down the ditch, in the direction from which he had just come, toward where the villagers had been.

"Stop, Ally!" Bird shouted at him, more than annoyed, but Ally only shoved with more determination, herding the children like sheep.

"We might as well go see what Ally's got in mind!" yelled Dren.

Just then Bird heard barking and realized the villagers must be coming back. She grabbed Ally's tail with both hands, dug in her heels, and tried to stop him, but the chimera just pulled her relentlessly forward, on and on, toward the barking. Issie and Dren, holding on to Bird's coat, were dragged along behind. The dogs barked louder. Bird was afraid, but she didn't want to lose Ally, so she held on. Next thing she knew, Ally brought them to a pack of dogs harnessed to a sled, with not a villager in sight. Everybody kissed and hugged Ally. Shouting to be heard above the storm, Bird made a plan: She would steer and Dren and Issie would ride.

The sled was as long as two men lying end to end, with a high bar at the back. Bird stood on the back and held on to the bar. How did you make a dogsled go? There weren't any reins. Bird saw Ally trying to bump the lead dog in the right direction. "Go!" shouted Bird. "Run! Go! Run!" shouted Issie and Dren. The dogs seemed frozen to the spot.

Bird trudged through the snow to the lead dog. "Go! Run!" she yelled in his ear. The dog just looked at her. What was wrong with these dogs?

She got back on the sled. "Go-go-go!" she yelled. "Forward, march!" Dren shouted. But nothing happened. "Please!" Issie wailed, in her most wheedling, plaintive voice, and to the children's great surprise, the dogs pulled the sled slowly into the snowy night. Ally led the way.

Soon they were whisking through the forest, the storm gentled by thick trees. Ally took the dogs in a switchback pattern up the ravine. He cut through the deep snow as if it were feathers. Sometimes, when the way became steeper, the dogs would stop, and the children would have to get off the sled and plod along beside it until the track was flatter again. Bird kept thinking of Stoke and wishing he were with them, wishing he wouldn't be so stubborn all the time. She tried to imagine he was still alive.

Finally the dogs stopped, and refused to move on even after the children climbed from the sled. Bird made her way forward to see what was the matter and stumbled right into the pony cart.

15

The Analari

Soladin never left her room. Its stone walls were carved as a forest, with lifelike pines, ferns, and woods' flowers. She continually ran her fingers over the intricate stone branches, the stone petals of marsh marigolds, the stone fur of a mouse.

—*A HISTORY OF WEN,* BY ISOGOLDE OF GILLADOOR

"**STOKE**! Stoke!" Bird shouted into the stormy night. Nobody answered. Issie and Dren shouted too. With sweeps of their arms, they easily removed the light dry snow from the cart. In no time at all, they uncovered sacks of food and sweaters, but no Stoke. The canvas they had used as a tent over the cart was gone too. Bird felt some relief. If Stoke had been under all that snow, he would have been frozen dead. He must have taken the canvas and made a shelter somewhere. But where?

"Stoke! Stoke!" she called. She was afraid and mad at the same time. If only he had come with them, or at least stayed with the wagon where they could find him. He always thought he knew what to do better than anybody.

"He's probably dead," moaned Issie. "It's all my fault. I shouldn't have insisted upon going into the village."

"No, it's not your fault. It's all his fault," said Bird.

Just then, Ally gave a roar and began windmilling his paws in the snow, burrowing under the cart. Bird and the others jumped to help him, and moments later they discovered a cave. Bird dove into it and tumbled onto Stoke, fast asleep.

She squashed snow in his face to wake him up. "I told you," said Stoke, after they recounted their adventures. "You should have stayed here." Dren and Issie squashed more snow in his face, until Stoke grumbled, "All right, all right, I won't say any more."

It was perfectly dark in Stoke's cave, even darker than outside. There wasn't enough room to sit up, so they lay down side-by-side, like sausages. Stoke had lined his cave with the canvas shelter cloth and some sweaters. With all four children, it was so warm they took off their fur robes. Finder found a spot in a corner near Bird's head. There wasn't room for Ally, but he seemed just as happy outside, piled in a heap with his new friends the sled dogs.

"Now we can get some sleep," said Issie, yawning.

"No we can't," said Stoke. "I just realized something: With all you've stirred up, we've got to move on. If we stay, they'll find us before morning."

"But I'm tired," said Issie, as if she were explaining something to a child, "and there's still a blizzard."

"And everybody who crosses the mountains in the winter dies," added Dren. "You keep forgetting to mention that part."

"I've been thinking about that," said Stoke. "I think we'll be fine. Nobody else has a chimera. Farwender and Ally sometimes crossed the Pokadoons in winter. I think this snow is just what we need. It'll make it hard for the villagers and Searchers to follow us. Besides, now we have a dogsled."

Bird had already laid her head on her star blanket. "Let's go in the morning. The villagers won't come after us in this storm."

"You might be right and you might be wrong," said Stoke. "If you're wrong, we're in big trouble."

"But what will we do with Apples?" she asked, already half asleep.

"We can leave her here. Someone will find her. We're right by the main road," said Stoke.

"What if no one sees her?" said Bird wearily. "The snow is too deep for her to get grass. She'll starve. You've already been sleeping, Stoke. Why don't you take Apples to the village and leave her in a barn. Ally can show you the way. We can go when you return." This sounded like an excellent idea to her, for she was already so sleepy she could barely talk. Her mind kept spinning words into dreams.

"Dren? Issie? What do you think?" asked Stoke. Nobody answered.

Next thing Bird knew, sometime much later that night, Stoke was gently waking her and the others, telling them Apples was safely in a barn. He said the storm had calmed, and he had been able to take the pony down the main road, without having to use Ally for a guide, which was just as well—no need to risk Ally again being seen by the villagers.

Stoke hadn't noticed any signs of the villagers hunting for them, but he thought they should leave right away, just in case. The exhausted children crawled from the warm cave and started packing. Working mostly by feel in the deep darkness, they loaded the long sled high and heavy, with no room for riders. Still they had to leave behind over half their baggage, including most of Farwender's sweaters and hats. They decided against taking any heavy food, such as apples and potatoes. Instead, they packed only journey bread—a dried mash of carrots, apricots, nuts, oats, and sheep grease. It tasted disgusting but was supposed to be long-lasting and nourishing. They covered the load with the shelter canvas, and lashed it down with rope. There wasn't any chocolate to pack—Stoke had gobbled it all while Bird and the others were gone.

By the time they harnessed the eight white dogs with curly tails, the wind had completely died down. Fat snowflakes drifted through the night sky. "Find Farwender," Bird instructed Ally. How Ally would know where Farwender was she had no idea, but Ally took off with a confident stride, and the eight dogs followed without even needing a "please." They seemed to have decided Ally was a worthy leader. Finder again rode in Ally's mane. The children walked on the hard-packed snow behind the sled. Almost immediately, Ally turned off the main road to go cross-country.

They labored on through the rest of the night, finally stopping mid-morning, when Dren spied the dark mouth of a cave that seemed unoccupied. They hauled the sled into it and slept in their furs with the animals piled around them. The dogs were wonderful heaters.

When the children woke, it was night again. They ate a bit of journey bread—not much because it had to last, who knew how long. Reluctantly, they offered journey bread to the animals as well. The dogs barked for more of the horrible stuff, but Ally and Finder wouldn't touch it. Bird guessed the chimera and cat had found mice in the back of the cave. Ally's snake tail loved mice as much as Finder did. The wind was howling again, like an angry warrior.

"Maybe we should wait until the storm calms down," said Issie.

"We'll run out of food and water if we wait," said Stoke, already harnessing the dogs.

They roped themselves together so they wouldn't lose anybody and trekked out into the icy darkness. Bird could barely see Issie, who was walking an arm's length in front of her. Everything was up to Ally.

Somewhere in the middle of the night, the trail became too steep for the dogs to pull the loaded sled. The children were already carrying light packs. They stuffed these with things from the sled until the dogs were able to go on. Their fur coats were heavy with ice and the wild winds drove ice splinters into their eyes whenever they opened them. They were too cold and miserable to complain that they were cold and miserable.

They took turns riding Ally, who seemed never to tire. Bird discovered they could use the Locket, which was always as warm as a new-laid egg, to unfreeze their feet and hands. The orphans took turns slipping it into their boots and mittens, which helped quite a bit.

Morning dawned gray and snowy. They stopped under an overhang of rock and concocted a shelter using the sled and canvas. "I can only find two water skins," said Bird, who was rummaging through the baggage for breakfast.

Stoke was cutting off chunks of journey bread for the dogs, who were all barking. "But we filled ten. Look again."

"I already looked again," said Bird. "There's only two, and they're both empty." She was suddenly thirstier than she had ever been in her life. She scooped some snow into her mouth.

"Don't do that," said Dren. "It'll freeze your insides. Next thing you know, you'll freeze to death."

"Frozen is better than thirsty." Bird put more snow in her mouth.

"I agree," said Issie, and she ate snow too.

"We could build a fire to melt snow, but there's no wood. We'd have to burn the sled," said Stoke.

Bird began to shiver. Dren was right about eating snow.

"I know," said Issie brightly. "The Locket!"

"Great idea, Iss," said Bird. They filled a pot with snow, put the Locket in it, and soon they had a puddle of water, enough for a few mouthfuls for everybody, including the animals. Then, leaving the Locket to melt more snow, they fell asleep.

When they woke up the next night, the storm was gone. The moon had not yet risen, and a zillion stars as sharp as needles filled a clean black sky. It was colder than ever, the air was still, and the peaks of the Pokadoons gleamed ghostly all around. Ally led them across a vast flank of mountain. The white dogs almost disappeared against the snow, but Ally's shaggy lion's head and black spotted body were easy to see as he trotted on and on, kicking up powdery snow clouds with his huge padded feet. Bird saw that Ally was now keeping his snake tail curled into an O, copying his new friends, the dogs.

Their way became ever steeper and again the dogs halted, unable to pull the sled. Grudgingly, the children unloaded their precious canvas shelter cloth and the rest of the sweaters, leaving only the sacks of journey bread on the sled. Then they set off again. Bird forced herself not to look back at the pile of castoffs.

The path grew even steeper. After a time, they were climbing more than walking, and the dogs stopped again. This time the dogs refused to continue until the children completely emptied the sled. The orphans put as much journey bread as each could carry into their rucksacks. Then they ate what they couldn't carry, feeding most of it to the hungry animals. According to Dren's calculations, they had enough journey bread for at least three more days, if they were careful.

The rest of the night they fought their way up and up. Ally seemed to be everywhere, encouraging them, and encouraging the dogs, who still pulled the empty sled. Bird was exhausted, and her hands and feet were frozen, despite using the Locket to warm them now and again. Her numb feet were clumsy, like poorly attached blocks of wood, and it was all she could do to keep herself from tumbling off the trail.

And then, as the sky lightened in the east, the trail ran smack-dab into a steep wall of rock. Bird could hardly believe it. Ally had led them to a dead end. She looked at the others, laden with heavy packs, and knew they could go no farther. But Ally immediately disappeared into a dark slit in the wall— even though he looked too big to fit through it.

The children stood there for a moment, stunned. Then Stoke said, "He's brought us this far. Let's keep following Ally." So they unharnessed the dogs—since the sled wouldn't fit through the crevice—and everybody, children and dogs, squeezed through the dark slit.

They found themselves in an enormous cavern, a huge
sculpted space of curves and domes and arches. The walls were
carved to seem like a stone forest, with life-sized trees, animals, and flowers. Pale winter's morning light poured down
through round portals. To Bird, it seemed they were in a wild
sort of palace.

"This must be the fastness of the Analari," said Stoke in a
hushed voice. "Like in the old stories. In ancient times, this is
where folk would come who were gravely ill in mind or spirit.
The Analari would care for them and anoint them with thalasse."

"Maybe some Analari are still here," said Issie. "Maybe they
could help us rescue Farwender, Soladin, and Piper. It would
be nice to have some help about now."

"I think I hear water," said Dren.

They discovered a thin waterfall, pouring from high on a
wall into a carved basin, and then flowing on through the cavern. Bird thought it was the most thirst-quenching liquid she
had ever tasted.

They found a storeroom stocked with rough cloth sacks of
nuts and dried fruit. They ate some right away. Then they
came upon a domed room with a tub, carved in the rock, fed
by a hot spring.

"Girls first," said Issie.

"No," said Dren. "You're too frozen. Your whole body will
burn with pain. First we need to thaw out by the fire."

It was hard to give up the bubbling tub, but Dren knew
more than any of them about medicine, because he was always
asking Soladin questions about it. The children returned to a

wide hall with a fireplace, which was large enough to roast a cow and already laid with wood. Stoke lit the fire with steel and flint and slowly, painfully, the children warmed their iced bodies. Then Bird and Issie stewed themselves in the hot spring until the heat seeped deep into their bones. Finally they were so hot they couldn't stand it; they had to get out of the tub. Bird had never felt so deliciously warm in her whole life. They put on thick woollen robes and socks from the storeroom.

After Dren and Stoke bathed, the children dragged giant sacks of feathers from the storeroom to the hall in front of the fire. They each had a feather sack for a mattress and another for a cover, and so were more comfortable than they had been since beginning their journey. They also arranged feather sacks for the animals, which were noisily gnawing on some discovered dried meat. As the children were falling asleep, Bird said, "Issie, if we ever get to have thalasse, what do you want from the Holder?"

Issie thought for a moment. "I want a gift for making people happy. So many people are sad. Maybe the Holder could give me special songs to sing, or stories. How about you?"

"I want to find my father. I've always wanted that more than anything." Bird fingered her star blanket. Lately she had begun to fear that maybe the star blanket had nothing to do with a father. Maybe the blanket was only to show folk she was the one who could open the Locket. But it was cut in half. The rest of it had to be somewhere, for some reason. "What do you want, Stoke and Dren?" she asked.

"I want to have a true heart, to always do what is right," said Stoke.

Dren said, "I'd like to be able to cross my eyes one at a time."
Everybody groaned.

"All right," said Dren. "I'll be serious. I'd like to make beautiful things, like the Wenish craftsfolk of old. Or maybe foretelling. It would fun to go around announcing what was going to happen next. But Farwender says one thing is for sure: The thalasse hardly ever gives anybody what they wish for."

Issie said, "That's because it gives them something better than they wish for."

Drifting into sleep, Bird wondered about what Issie had said. How could the thalasse give her something better than a real father—to protect her, tell her stories, hold her?

The children slept all afternoon. However, one time Bird woke to hear what sounded like someone laughing, as happily as she had ever heard—a sound that made her think of a silk banner unfurling in the wind, loose and shimmering. She thought it might be one of the winged Analari. She scrambled from her bed and ran toward the sound, but it ceased at once. She was left with a yearning to hear it again, like the hunger she had to hear Farwender's voice.

The orphans would have loved to stay in the caverns, at least until the snow melted, but the fate of Farwender, Soladin, and Piper lay upon them, and after a day and a night, with fresh provisions from the storeroom, they continued their journey. Since they were surely alone in the mountains, they decided it would be safe to travel by day. They set out into a dazzling world of sun, blue sky, and snow.

The carven caverns were at the crest of the mountain range, and for a time they traveled on a long high ridge, with the flanks of the mountain dropping away on both sides. Other mountains rose all around, and it was as if they rode the top of a wave in a sea of giant frozen waves. Then it was down and down, for several days. The dogs, barking joyously, pulled the children in the sled, so fast at times that the snow plumed behind them. Finally the snow thinned and disappeared. They sold the sled, dogs, and fur robes to a goat farmer and walked on, each one of them feeling the great strength that comes to folk when they endure and survive trials. Bird felt more powerful than a giant.

The children felt so strong that they left off some of their earlier fear and wariness. The goat farmer had told them they were in the land of Wen, yet far from its capital. He hadn't seen soldiers of any sort for years, he said. So the children decided they were safe enough; they might as well continue to travel by day. They were quite noticeable in Farwender's rainbow sweaters.

Ally continued to lead them. The children had always respected the chimera, but now that he had taken them across the Pokadoon Mountains in a snowstorm to the strange carven caverns, they knew that he was truly a magical beast. Finder seemed to agree, as she persisted in riding on top of Ally's head, even though there was no snowstorm to shelter from.

After a few days, the travelers came to a path along a stream, which soon became a road beside a river. In time, they saw a man, fishing in the river. When he saw them, he waved his hands madly over his head and shouted, "At last, at last, you've come."

16

A Feast of Pulpatoons

*Soladin saw stern pride run into Rendarren's face. "I am Ren-
darren, son of Rondel. I have never bowed to anyone, but I bow
to you, milady, for I see that you hold both beauty and power
within you as lightly as birdsong." Then Rendarren knelt, lowered his dark head, and offered her his sword, with its long
curved edge.*

—*A HISTORY OF WEN,* BY ISOGOLDE OF GILLADOOR

THE fisherman, a plump fellow with a round red face, said his
name was Nippy. He explained he was from Paradoona, a village of Wenish folk still faithful to the Tree That Speaks. "I
know it must be hard to trust folk, after all you have been
through," Nippy said. "Perhaps this will help." He offered them
his palm so they could see it bore the scar of an X. Oddly for a
fisherman, Nippy was dressed in fine clothes, a brown velvet
tunic over black velvet baggy leggings. He told them the mayor
of his village had set him to watch a week ago, when news
reached the village of Farwender and Soladin's fate, and the
rewards offered for the Locket, the chimera, and the skinny
girl. The mayor figured the chimera and the girl might try to
cross the mountains, looking for Farwender.

"Am I glad to see you," said Nippy. "We thought for sure
you perished in that awful storm. I don't see how you made it.

But here you are, safe at last!" Nippy laughed anxiously, like a person about to be tickled. "Please accept my invitation on behalf of Paradoona to honor us with a visit. Let us feast and entertain you." He tittered again.

The children moved apart from Nippy to discuss what to do. Bird, Issie, and Dren were sure it was a good idea to go with him, because of the X scar on his hand. Stoke was the only one with doubts. "How could there be a village loyal to the Tree so close to Rendarren's stronghold?"

"But Nippy's on our side," said Bird. "He's got that scar. Maybe somehow his village pretends to go along with Rendarren, but secretly they're rebels. Maybe they could help us rescue Farwender and Soladin."

"Nippy's laugh gives me the heebie-jeebies," said Stoke.

"Lots of people have annoying habits, but good hearts," said Issie. "Look at Farwender, the way he spits when he talks." Everybody laughed and decided to follow Nippy to Paradoona.

All afternoon, Nippy led them downstream through steep, forested hills, until they came to a town built of stone. They crossed into the town on a wide turreted bridge, and then continued up a cobbled street. The town seemed prosperous, with big stone houses and well-tended gardens. Folk dressed in dark velvet waved at Nippy from rose gardens and wide porches. The orphans and their guide walked to the top of the hill, where stood the grandest house of all, a many-storied mansion much bigger than the lordhouse where Bird had lived in Graynok. They passed through a tall gate of iron scrollwork, climbed dozens of stairs, and finally arrived at a massive front door carved with laughing faces.

Nippy struck a small gong. As they waited for someone to answer, Bird looked out over the prosperous town. She felt quite in awe of Paradoona, but it did seem odd that Rendarren's enemies could live so elegantly right under his nose. Her stomach scrunched nervously. To calm her fears, she kept thinking of the scar on Nippy's hand.

A servant girl invited them to wait in a marble entry room lined with tall mirrors. "Don't we look awful," whispered Issie to Bird, pointing at their ragged, dirty reflections.

Right then, a middle-aged man even plumper than Nippy arrived. The food here must be worth eating, thought Bird. The new man was dressed all in purple velvet, including a puffy purple cap with red feathers sticking up on both sides like rabbit's ears. Nippy bowed low before him. "Sebeelyo, honored head. I present to you these wanderers, our cousins from afar, and their marvelous beast."

"Welcome, welcome," said Sebeelyo in a warm voice that sounded as if it often told jokes. "A chimera! How amazing to actually see a chimera! I've only heard of them in stories." Sebeelyo reached out to tousle Ally's mane, only to have Finder pop up her head and snarl. Sebeelyo jumped back, but then he laughed and said, "And a cat! How nice! I simply love cats, especially white ones."

After dismissing Nippy with much praise, Sebeelyo had the children remove their boots and the servant girl wipe the paws of Finder and Ally, plus the mud on the marble floor. He asked for the children's names, which he said carefully a few times each, as if to fix them in his mind. Then he led them down a hall where the carpet was thicker than chimera fur. Arched windows looked over the town and river.

Issie said, "I hope you don't mind our appearance. We've been on the road for many days, and I'm afraid we've lacked proper bathing facilities, for the most part."

Sebeelyo chuckled again. At least, thought Bird, he has a nicer laugh than that fellow Nippy. "My dear, how unthinking of me," Sebeelyo said. "You are so beautiful I didn't even notice your dirt. But surely it would be only kind of me to hold my curiosity and allow you to wash up." He rang a silver bell, and the serving girl reappeared. "Please show our guests to their chambers, and have the tubs filled in their rooms, if you would, my dear."

"What about Ally and Finder?" asked Bird, surprised that Sebeelyo had allowed the animals into his grand house.

"Oh, I know it seems fancy here, but you'll find that it's really as homey as an old pair of slippers. I love having animals in the house," Sebeelyo said, and dismissed them all with a twinkling wave of his tiny fat fingers, each decorated with a jeweled ring or two.

The servant girl led them up a dark carved staircase to what seemed about the fourth floor. There was a separate room for each child. Where had all the money for this mansion come from? Bird wondered. Her room was decorated in pink, with a huge bed draped in pink silk and laden with pillows of cream silk. Ally, with Finder walking beside him, followed Bird into her room. The chimera sniffed under the bed and behind the curtains, and finally, apparently satisfied there were no spies, settled on the white furs by the fire. Finder began a nap nearby.

The servant girl searched through a wardrobe and took out a long dress of pink silk and cream lace and a pair of silk slippers to match. Bird had hardly even seen silk before in her life; she barely knew what it was, and here it was everywhere. She reached out to touch the dress, but then saw how grimy her hand was and thought better of it. She was so dirty, she was afraid to sit down anywhere, so she remained standing as the girl filled the tub, added drops of rose scent, strewed fresh rose petals across the water, and left.

Bird peeled off her rainbow sweater, which somewhere in the mountains had lost the yellow pom-pom from its hood. She removed her pink tunic embroidered with strawberries, which Soladin had made her, and her underclothes, but she left the Locket on. She piled her clothes on the wood floor, where she figured they wouldn't soil anything. Then she climbed into the tub. Her sore, dirty body relaxed in the warm water as the scent of roses filled her nostrils.

Bird wanted to soak forever, but she knew Sebeelyo was eager to hear of their adventures. She dried herself with the plush cloth that lay folded on a bench by the tub, and then fixed her hair with a silver brush and comb, quickly braiding it into a crown, as Soladin had taught her.

The pink silk dress fit perfectly, and the pink satin slippers too, with their ribbon fastenings. The lace edge of the long full skirt swept the floor. Bird twirled and then gasped as she caught her reflection in a full-length mirror. She looked fragile and graceful, more beautiful than ever before in her life. Her waist, with a huge pink bow tied behind, looked delicate and small. It was hard to believe it was really herself, Bird.

She tucked the Locket under the lacy silk bodice. "Come on, Ally," she said. "I'm sure he'll have lots of questions about you." Yawning and stretching, Ally rose to follow her. Even he seemed affected by their luxurious surroundings. Finder looked at Bird as if to say, "Surely he won't be interested in me," and so Bird let her stay drowsing before the fire.

Evening had come, and the grand house was softly lit with candles. As Bird ran down the stairs, she heard her friends laughing with Sebeelyo, and she followed the sound to find them in a cozy sitting room to one side of the grand hall. "Ah, Bird, my dear," said Sebeelyo, rising to greet her. He took her hand and kissed it. He led her to a cushioned chair and presented her with a small glass of something warm and bittersweet, which she had never tasted before.

Her friends also were transformed by their new clothing. Issie wore a gown of blue, which floated around her, ruffles upon ruffles. Her yellow curls were caught up on top of her head with a big blue bow. Dren looked handsome but a little silly in his velvet leggings and silk shirt with flowing sleeves. Stoke, in a long black velvet coat, was Bird's idea of a young lord. Bird found herself relaxing in the warmth of Sebeelyo's charm and hospitality. She thought there was a good chance Sebeelyo would help them with their rescue plans. She could see that Dren and Issie felt the same way. They looked happy and satisfied, but Stoke had his mouth set in a way that meant he was feeling stubborn about something.

Soon Sebeelyo led them into the dining chamber for something he called "a feast of pulpatoons"—hundreds of small intricate treats piled on silver platters to form flowers or castles or butterflies. Everything was crunchy or sweet or juicy or flaky or dripping with butter or all those things at once. It was the most delicious food Bird had ever put in her mouth. Ally had his own silver bowl of pulpatoons, which was constantly replenished as he gobbled them down. It was only when everyone was stretching back and saying, "I couldn't eat another bite," or, "I hope my stomach doesn't pop," that Sebeelyo began to ask questions.

Stoke, who usually liked to do the important talking, hung back from speaking, and gave the others his "shut up" glare. Even though she found this annoying, Bird decided to honor Stoke by holding her tongue until they could talk privately. But Issie recounted to Sebeelyo their entire story, ending with, "So we're going to try to rescue Soladin, Farwender, and Piper."

"We just might be able to do it," said Dren. "We already made it over the Pokadoons in a blizzard."

Sebeelyo leaned forward. The joking look on his face had disappeared, to be replaced by a warm and serious expression. "I know Farwender and Soladin must be as parents to you, so I find this hard to say. But look at you. Four children—two of you girls. Your idea is noble. I admire it. It's always good to dream. But how can you hope to outwit Rendarren's army? Even I and all the strong men of my village would be no match for them."

"I'm as strong as most boys," said Bird.

"But not as most men," said Sebeelyo. "Farwender is Rendarren's brother and Soladin has been sweetheart to both. It is an ugly family quarrel which no one can do anything about. We can only hope that they will work it out among themselves."

"There's something much more important at stake, actually," said Issie. "Stop kicking me, Stoke! We have the Locket that holds the Seed with us. We want to plant a new Tree That Speaks. Maybe you could help us."

Sebeelyo pushed back in his chair and stroked his triple chin with a bejeweled hand. "I'd like to help, but I cannot. The people of Paradoona gave up warfare some time ago. Besides, I hardly think I should persuade my people to die just so you can rescue your friends and plant a tree."

"Not just *a* tree. The Tree That Speaks. Don't you want it to grow again?" asked Bird.

"That's a good question, young lady, a very good question. You see, I was a young man when the Tree fell, and I tell you, it was a terrible time. The Tree was a symbol of all we were and hoped for, and it was dead. Rendarren's warriors killed my parents. I fled with others into a high mountain valley. Over half of us died that winter. It came to those of us who survived that if the Holder really existed, He would have spoken to us, or protected us from Rendarren, or something. He wouldn't have abandoned us. As time passed, we left the old ways, timidly at first and then wholeheartedly.

"I remember the first time I went to bed without giving thanks to the Holder. I don't know what I expected, perhaps a giant hand coming down from the sky and shaking its finger at me." Sebeelyo grinned. "But nothing happened.

"One day, Rendarren discovered us. By that time, I was

mayor—we had abandoned the old title of watchman—watching for what? I admit that at this point, I was tempted to call out to the Holder for help, but I did not. Instead, I sent emissaries to Rendarren, asking his terms for peace. I knew his ruthless reputation, but I figured it wouldn't hurt to try. To my surprise and delight, he was willing to leave us be. The only thing he asked was that we cease to keep the light of Wen."

Here the four travelers looked at each other in horror. Farwender had drilled into them that it was the sworn duty of the watchman or watchwoman of each village, great or small, to keep a light of Wen always shining, so all would know where to go for help. Farwender had kept the light on his porch brightly lit even though he lived in bandit country, and knew Rendarren was scouring the earth to find him. Bird thought about how Farwender's light had guided her the night Piper lay dying.

"I see you are distressed at the idea," said Sebeelyo, looking down at his plate as if embarrassed. "I was too, at first, to tell the truth. But imagine the choice. Our town burned to the ground. People I loved dying. Or merely to blow out a light on my front porch."

"When you look at it that way, it does sound reasonable," said Issie. Bird was amazed to hear her say this.

Sebeelyo smiled at Issie. "Just because I blew it out didn't mean I would stop helping people. People could still find my house, and I could still be as helpful and hospitable as ever—as I have to you this night! So, yes, I blew out the light. I did feel a little funny when Rendarren insisted that I blow it out with great ceremony, with the entire town watching, and all of his army standing by. I had thought perhaps I could just let it quietly burn out. But anyway, I did it, and do you know what? The people gave out a great cheer.

"Since then, life has continued to improve for us. As an unexpected favor, Rendarren moved us from our barren hideaway to this hillside. He had this house—or I should say mansion—built for me. Our whole village has become exceedingly wealthy, and Rendarren only taxes us the smallest amount. It's the most miraculous thing. I imagine he must be greatly changed from the days of his youth."

While Sebeelyo talked, Stoke had been rubbing his X scar with the thumb of his other hand, around and around. Now he lifted his head and said in a carefully offhand way, "So you are not about to help us with the Seed?"

"Well, no. You see, I promised Rendarren we wouldn't fight him anymore. And I am nothing if not a man of my word."

"But don't you want to restore the Tree That Speaks to Wen, and experience the thalasse? Doesn't your heart cry to know the Holder?" asked Stoke.

"I can't really say my heart is crying for anything," said Sebeelyo, with a happy sigh. "I am quite content as I am."

"But you are willing to put us up in your house in this glorious manner," Stoke said.

"For a while. We are brothers, even if we differ in our views of our heritage."

"Have you told Rendarren that we're here?" asked Stoke.

"The Holder bless me, no! What do you take me for, a traitor? And I do beg you all to stay at least a week. Issie my darling, you especially. You are so lovely in that blue dress. We will be having a small ball tomorrow night, and I'm sure my son would love to dance with you."

Issie smiled, but then asked, "Let me make sure I understand. You see no point in planting the Seed."

"Ah, the Seed. Which one of you has it?" Sebeelyo looked intently from child to child.

Despite Stoke's glaring at her, Issie said, "Bird does. She's probably got it on right now."

Sebeelyo turned his moist brown eyes on Bird. "So you are the Opener, the Child wrapped in sparrow song? How delightful. I don't suppose you would be kind enough to show the Seed to me? I've heard so many stories about it—that it gives off a shower of light that heals headaches and warts, that it makes music and turns lead into gold."

"It does give a light," said Bird. "But I've never seen any of the other things happen." She looked over at Stoke.

Stoke shrugged his shoulders. "Show it to him. Maybe then he'll believe."

Bird walked over to their host. She pulled out the Locket, leaving the chain around her neck for safety. "All right," she said as she opened it, "have a look." The Seed appeared as a tiny flame with rainbow edges.

Sebeelyo stared at it. "But my dear," he said, looking up at her with pity, "there's nothing there!"

"You can't see it?" asked Bird, in disbelief, as the flame burned higher.

"I see a bed of green moss with a tiny glass vial on it. But the vial is completely empty. If there ever were a Seed, it's gone now. How sad for you all."

"But there's a tiny flame. I can feel its heat in the palm of my hand," said Bird.

"I see it," said Stoke.

"Me too," said Issie.

"A flame," said Dren.

"Strange," said Sebeelyo, shaking his head. "Strange how one sees what one wants to see. Would anyone care for dessert?"

Dessert was served, six different kinds. Sebeelyo had a bit of each and Issie daintily nibbled at a cream puff, but the rest of the children ate nothing at all. Sebeelyo talked on as before, laughing and asking interesting questions and telling jokes. Issie obliged him with giggling and constant chatter, but to the others, his graciousness seemed a hollow thing, a rattling in the wind.

17

ESCAPE

"You are beautiful," he said, in a deep and certain voice.

I had often heard of my beauty. Various lords and prince-lings who wished to marry me had composed songs and poems about it. Farwender continually driveled on about it, but still, I didn't know I was beautiful until that moment, when Rendarren fastened his eyes on me and said, "You are beautiful." Then I knew my beauty from the top of my head to the tips of my toes, and I marveled at its power over the hearts of men, especially over this one man, whom I craved beyond all others. Yes, I was beautiful. He said so.

—*CONFESSIONS,* BY SOLADIN LEAFSTAR, TREEKEEPER OF WEN

ISSIE seemed to have a million things to say to Sebeelyo before she said good night. They finally left for their rooms, but Bird had to pull on Issie's arm all the way up the stairs to keep her from going back to talk more to their plump host. Once they were upstairs, Stoke immediately dismissed the ever-present servants and called a council in his room.

They sat on furs close to the fire and whispered, with only the flickering flames to light their faces. Ally took guard position, lying across the door. Bird rubbed her face, trying to dispel her after-dinner grogginess.

"We're in a trap," said Stoke. "That Sebeelyo's on Rendarren's side. I'll bet he's already sent a messenger to Rendarren. We've got to get out of here as soon as possible."

"He said he isn't a traitor, and I believe him," said Issie.

"Excuse me," said Stoke, "were you listening? He extinguished the light of Wen."

"I am sorry he did that," said Issie, arranging her skirt in a puff around her. "He seems misguided here and there. But I can understand how it was hard for him to choose between his people dying and some old light. It's an understandable mistake, if you ask me, although I wouldn't do it myself."

"Stop it!" said Bird. "We don't have time to argue. We need to get out of here fast!"

Dren said, "Maybe he isn't a traitor, maybe he is. But there are too many things that aren't quite right around here. You've got to see that, Issie."

"If he's so bad, why did he feed us a big, tasty dinner?" said Issie. "Why didn't he just lock us up?"

"He's just playing with us until Rendarren gets here," said Stoke.

"You're too suspicious about everything," said Issie. "Let's go to bed and talk about it in the morning."

Stoke's face went grim. "We might be dead by morning."

Issie gave a big sniff. "It's fine for you all to go running off into the night. You're all healthy. But look at me. My nose will not stop running, and I think I've got a fever. I need at least a day to rest up. Do you have a handkerchief, Dren?"

Bird said, "You just want to go to that ball and dance with Sebeelyo's son."

"It wouldn't bother me to go to a ball," said Issie. She blew her nose into Dren's handkerchief. "Of course, I can see where a ball wouldn't appeal to you, Bird. No fighting or biting. Anyway, it would be a miracle from the Holder if anyone asked you to dance." Issie turned to Dren. "How about you, Dren? What about one more day? I'd love to dance with you."

"One more day might be all right," mumbled Dren.

"Dren!" said Bird, forgetting to whisper. "Don't you see what Issie's doing? She's flirting with you so you'll do what she wants."

"Shush your mouth," said Issie. "I am not. Dren and I have been special friends since childhood."

Stoke interrupted. "Enough. Every moment we delay places us in greater danger. You aren't that sick, Issie. Let's vote. I say go."

"Go," said Bird.

Dren wearily dropped his head. "Go," he said.

"Oh, donkey poop," said Issie.

Stoke jumped to his feet. "Change back to your old clothes, get your rucksacks, and meet again here. Quick."

With a growing sense that something evil lurked in the grand house, Bird hastily returned to her room. She strained her ears, listening for the slightest noise, but heard nothing. She changed clothes and packed fast. At least her boots had been returned to her room; silk slippers would be terrible for running through the forest. With Ally and Finder right beside her, she was back in Stoke's room before the others.

"What are we going to do about Issie?" she muttered as they waited in the darkness.

"She'll be fine once we get free of this place," said Stoke. "At least she went along with the vote."

"I was afraid she was going to throw a fit and wake up the whole house."

"I know she was hard on you," said Stoke, "but can't you see you're jealous?"

"I am not," Bird whispered angrily.

"Yes you are. You wish you were as beautiful as she is."

"Oh, come on," said Bird, as Stoke's words sliced into her heart. She knew what he said was true. But for Stoke, of all people, to say it, when he was so handsome and she liked him so much.

"You know I'm right," said Stoke. There was an awkward silence, and then Dren and Issie slipped into the room.

They considered leaving the mansion by climbing down a tree near Stoke's window, but it was an impossible leap to the nearest branch. So they decided to go out by the front door, since they didn't know any other way. The children and their animals snuck down the grand staircase, the deep carpet silencing their footsteps. The hall was empty. They made their way to the door. Still no one was about. Sebeelyo apparently was not expecting or interested in stopping their escape. Bird began to wonder if Sebeelyo was really as bad as they thought.

Stoke raised the door latch. The door gave a long creak as he pulled it open, and the four children froze in place, listening to see if anyone heard and came. No one did. They moved out onto the dark portico.

Below them, the town rested in the deep quietness of night, in the weak light of a half moon. The children tiptoed down the multitude of stairs to the wide stone path to the gate. The big gate, with its scrolled ironwork, was locked, but a smaller gate in the hedge nearby was a crack open. They sped through it and found themselves at last free of the house of Sebeelyo. But as they looked around in a moment of relief and congratulation, they realized Issie was missing.

"She must be back at the house," said Stoke.

"I bet her hair got mussed, and she's combing it," said Bird.

"I'm going to check," said Stoke. "Stay here."

"No. I'll go," said Dren. "If I don't come back soon, you two leave without me."

"Let's all go look for her," said Bird. "We shouldn't split up."

"No," said Stoke, "Dren's right. We've got to protect the Seed. Look, Dren—Bird and I will go to the bridge. If you're not back by the time we sing 'Wen Arise' ten times, we'll go on without you, the same trail as before, downriver."

Dren nodded, then disappeared back through the gate. Staying in shadows, Bird, Stoke, Ally, and Finder made their way to the turreted bridge and hid themselves the best they could in the riverbank scrub. With their backs against Ally's warm fur, and Finder purring in Bird's lap, the two friends sang as they had promised, with the river murmuring an accompaniment. Stoke held up one more finger each time they finished the song.

"Let Wen arise, and her people grow bolder; let Wen arise, to right all wrong; let Wen arise and remember the Holder; let Wen arise and sing her song."

They sang in whispers, and with every verse, they sang more slowly. It was unthinkable to Bird to go on without their companions. Even though Issie was acting like a priss, she didn't deserve to fall into the hands of an evil fake like Sebeelyo, or worse yet, Rendarren.

It seemed to Bird they had been singing forever when finally Stoke put up nine fingers. By unspoken agreement, they slowed their singing even more, but when they finished the song, they were still alone.

Bird stroked Finder. "We can't just leave them."

"We don't have a choice," said Stoke. "The Seed comes first."

"We can't let Rendarren get them. I'm going back."

18

ALLY'S BATTLE

I pulled my horse to a rearing halt. There was the Tree, and circled around it as in all the tales were the lion-snake beasts named chimeras. It is written that he who would fell the Tree must first slay the chimeras, so I leaped from my horse, drew my sword, and rushed yelling at the largest. The beast received the death-blow without moving or making a sound. So it was with his companions. One by one I severed their heads, yet those who remained alive stood still and silent as vegetables, except for their eyes, which followed me as I worked. I finished exhausted and covered with their thick purple blood. The pleasure of killing is greatly diminished when the victim lacks the courage to fight.

—THE DEATH OF THE TREE, BY LORD RENDARREN OF WEN

THE animals close on her heels, Bird burst from the bushes and with all her strength ran up the steep rock street, trying not to be afraid of what might happen next. She couldn't let Rendarren hurt her friends; Farwender would want her to save them if she could. Before long, she heard Stoke's feet pounding beside her own. They came to Sebeelyo's mansion, slipped through the side gate, and ran up the path and portico stairs. The front door was still unlocked, and when Bird opened it, it gave a long creak, as before.

The mirrored entry hall was dark and empty, but she heard

gruff voices upstairs. Quietly, Bird sped up the stairs, with Stoke, Ally, and Finder at her heels. The door to Issie's room was open. As they approached it, Ally growled, then leaped past Bird into the room. Bird's heart beat faster, but she didn't hesitate. She rushed into the room right behind the chimera.

"Hello," said Sebeelyo, in the same charming, cheerful voice with which he had suggested they take a bath before dinner. "We've been hoping you might come, my dears." In the flickering firelight, Bird could see that the room was filled with soldiers—not Searchers, but some other kind of soldiers wearing hats that looked like buckets. Some of them held swords to the throats of Issie and Dren. Ally was facing the soldiers, growling low.

Bird and Stoke turned to escape down the stairs, but more soldiers blocked their way. Sebeelyo's gracious-host voice continued. "To think you almost caught me napping! But Issie woke me, stumbling on the stairs, and so I rang the alarm. I had thought you were spending the night! I am sorry to capture you, truly I am, but you must see, my dears, that four children, strangers to me, are hardly worth the lives of the folk of Paradoona. And when Rendarren said he wanted you, well, that was enough for me. And of course, there are the rewards." Sebeelyo pointed at Bird and Stoke. "Arrest them. Take the necklace off the dark-haired girl and give it to me."

The soldiers grabbed Stoke and Bird. Sebeelyo began to walk out of the room, but he never got through the door. With an awful roar, Ally sprang on him and tore out his throat. Quickly Ally turned to attack the soldiers holding Bird. His snake tail bit one soldier while his lion's mouth bit another, and just like that, she was free. Then Ally rushed this way and that, maiming and wounding the screaming soldiers, leaping, biting, crashing, knocking over furniture, ripping flesh and feather pillows with his claws. Soon the other three children were free as well, and all four of them hid behind a plump silk couch not far from the door.

They would have run out the door, but more soldiers were pouring through it, intent upon rescuing their comrades. Ally took on the new batch of soldiers with such fierceness that most of them ran out of the room screaming.

But then, as Bird watched from their hiding place, a soldier swiped Ally's side with his sword, opening a dreadful wound. Another soldier cut a long gash on Ally's neck. Bird began to fear for Ally's life. She wanted to help him, but she was terrified—the soldiers were whacking with swords longer than she was. What if the Locket didn't protect her from death after all? She'd never tested it. And she was weaponless, except for the scissor-blade knife in her boot.

Ally killed more soldiers, then paused, panting. The three soldiers who remained, sensing the chimera weakening, closed around him for the kill. Ally rushed at one of them with a mighty yowl, leaving him in a bloody heap. But then, another soldier, with a deft slice, managed to cut off Ally's snake tail. Bird's whole body clenched in grief. While his tail writhed helplessly on the floor, Ally raged on, but Bird could see he was losing strength. His leaps were shorter and awkward now. Surely, she knew, Ally would die without his tail. The two remaining soldiers began to taunt him, trying to provoke the chimera toward them so they could finish him off. Ally backed farther and farther toward the windows, away from the door.

"Quick," said Stoke. "Ally's distracting them away from us. Go!" Issie and Dren jumped over Sebeelyo's dead body in the doorway and dashed down the stairs. When Bird made no move to leave, Stoke grabbed her arm to pull her after him, but she jerked from his grasp. She was not leaving Ally to die.

"We've got to help him," she cried.

"We can't help him. We'll be killed," Stoke cried back.

Bird ran from behind the couch. Using both hands, she picked up a broadsword she saw glinting in the firelight and struck at the nearest soldier with all her might. The blade bounced off the man's chest armor, and he laughed, but then he stopped laughing as Ally knocked him over. The man and the chimera struggled on the floor for a moment, and then Ally staggered to his paws. The man was dead.

Bird turned to see the other soldier coming toward her. Strength flooded her body. "In the name of the light of Wen," she shouted, and swung hard, only to have her weapon clang against her enemy's and be violently knocked from her hands. The soldier, only three arm's lengths away, raised his sword to kill her. Bird hoped the Locket would protect her, but in case it didn't, she got ready. She dropped to a crouch and pulled the scissor blade from her boot. Gripping it, she prepared to fling herself forward and stab the man on his unprotected face the minute he lunged for her. But the soldier never struck his blow. Instead, there was a terrible roar, such as a firestorm makes devouring grasslands. Ally hurled himself at the soldier and, with a tinkling splintering of glass, leaped through the window, pushing the man out before him.

Bird ran to the window. In the soft moonlight, she could

barely make out two dark, motionless forms on the ground many stories below. She could not tell if either the man or Ally lived. People were yelling and running in the house. Probably more soldiers were coming.

"Come on." Stoke grabbed her again. This time she went with him. In the confusion and darkness of the alarmed household, they managed to run down all the stairs, through the hall, out the front door, and down the portico steps without being stopped. Stoke never loosened his grip on Bird's arm. But at the bottom of the steps, as Stoke pulled her toward the little gate, she wrenched out of his hold.

"I'm going to Ally," she yelled back at him as she sped away. "Maybe he's still alive."

The others had never appreciated Ally, she thought as she raced. Nobody loved him rightly but her. Careening around the corner of the house, she saw in the distance two dark mounds on the lawn. She ran faster. She came to Ally. His mouth was hugely open. His eyes were cold dark glass. She knew he was dead. She grabbed his giant furry head with all of her strength and hugged him to her. She stroked his mane, the tangled rough fur of it, and wept.

Somebody pulled at her arm. It was Stoke, begging her to come with him. She heard him as if he spoke across mountains and hills and oceans. She felt him lift the weight of Ally's head from her arms.

"You must come," he whispered fiercely in her ear. "Think of the rest of us. Think of the Seed. Think of Farwender, Soladin, Piper."

"No! No!" she wailed.

"Yes. Do it for Ally," he insisted.

At Ally's name, Bird woke to life again. She shrugged off Stoke's helping hands and ran with him, crying as she ran, around the house, through a back gate, down pathways this way and that. Everywhere, alarm bells clanged. Stoke veered off the path and Bird followed, plunging through shrubbery and then running along the river, stumbling over weeds and rubble, to the bridge, to its dark pointed towers. Dren and Issie were waiting there, near the boat dock, Issie holding Finder.

Bird held out her arms, and Finder leaped into them.

"Ally?" asked Issie.

"Dead," said Bird.

"Poor, poor Ally," said Issie, covering her face with her hands, shaking her head as if that would make the truth go away. "It's my fault he died. I did everything wrong. I'm so, so sorry."

"Sure you are," said Bird.

"Stop it!" said Stoke. "It's over! We have to get out of here. Let's take that boat!" Stoke began frantically untying the mooring ropes of a nearby boat, while the rest of the children tumbled into it. They could hear people shouting, coming closer, the alarm bells jangling on. The knot gave way. Stoke jumped into the boat. Dren grabbed a long pole from the bottom of the boat and pushed them out into the main current of the river. "Lie flat," ordered Stoke, and they all did. The current swept them away.

For the rest of the night, they rode the deep swift river, passing through an increasingly tall, dense forest. Now and again, they drifted toward the shore, and Dren had to use his pole to push them back into the main channel, but for the most part, the boat floated onward unassisted. Sometimes they sped faster over gentle rapids, but they never encountered violent waters. At first, the orphans listened anxiously for the sounds of pursuit, for beating hooves on the riverbank, or shouts from a galley, but nothing came. Somehow, they had escaped. They slept.

As the night wore on, Bird wandered in and out of sleep. She dreamed of her life with Soladin, Ally, and Finder in the river cottage, only to wake to the ever-fleeing walls of dark forest. Then she remembered that Ally was dead, and wept, and fell asleep again. Finally, she entered a sleep beyond dreams.

She was woken by Finder, purring and weaving her small body back and forth against her face. Finder was hungry. Bird cuddled the cat to her, looking about the boat for food, but there was none. They had left their rucksacks behind.

At least the forest was a more friendly green in the morning light. Bird looked at the others; they were still sleeping. Underneath Issie's arm, tightly held and crumpled, she saw a wad of blue. Issie's fancy blue dress. Why did Issie have that dress? The reason exploded in Bird's mind: Issie had gone back to get it. If she had not gone back to get that dress, Ally would be alive.

Bird yanked the dress out from under Issie's arm. Its blue silk was bloody and ripped. Issie woke with a start, screaming and clutching to grab the dress back, but Bird spun away and flung it into the river, as far from the boat as she could. The dress floated in the water like a huge blue flower.

19

Rendarren's Eyes

Everywhere one looked, there was beauty and mystery. Thick chartreuse moss carpeted the forest floor, mist scarves wove among the pines, and waves flung themselves upon the sea cliffs in splendid abandon.

—*A HISTORY OF WEN,* BY ISOGOLDE OF GILLADOOR

ISSIE screamed as if someone had ripped off her arm. Bird couldn't stand it. She knocked Issie to the bottom of the boat and pumped her fists into her face. Issie just lay there, screeching, not even trying to fight back, which made Bird angrier, made her hit harder. The boat was wide and shallow, more a raft than a boat, and it rocked crazily with the struggle.

Dren woke and shouted, "Stoke! Bird's killing Issie!" The boys crawled across the floor of the pitching boat to the girls, pulled them apart, and fell back. Dren held a sobbing Issie at one end of the boat while Stoke gripped a flailing Bird in the other. Issie's nose streamed blood.

"Let me go," Bird demanded. Stoke tightened his grip on her arm, which he had winched behind her back so it hurt to move.

"She tried to kill me," sobbed Issie. "If you hadn't rescued me, I would be dead."

"Big wody-dody," said Bird. "Can't take a few fists in the

face. What about poor Ally? You killed him. You deserve to be dead." She spat.

Stoke grunted with the effort of holding Bird down. "You could have had us in the river!"

"She threw my dress in the river. I want my dress." Issie wailed louder. The dress had snagged on a dead branch and was now the merest speck of blue far upstream.

Dren put a long arm around Issie's shoulders. "Please, Issie, stop crying. Your dress is gone. When could you have worn it anyway? We're not going to a ball anytime soon."

"I know," said Issie, sobbing between words. "I know what you all think. I made Ally die. I'm sorry. I'm sorry. Haven't you ever made a terrible mistake?"

Dren patted Issie's shoulder. "You didn't mean for Ally to die. Don't worry, we understand."

"Ally is dead," said Bird, yearning to hit Issie again. "I've never made a mistake that bad. I'll never forgive you." She spat at Issie again.

"Bird," said Stoke firmly. "Forgive and forget, like Farwender says."

At Stoke's words, anger flushed through Bird as a heat from her toes to her head. "Yeeeeeeowww!" she yelled, lunging free of Stoke's grip to fall on Issie. She bit the first part of Issie that came near her mouth, a cheek. She bit hard, and tasted the richness of warm blood. Issie screamed.

Stoke grabbed Bird by both braids and hauled her to her feet. "Stop it!"

"No," Bird cried, flailing her arms and kicking at Stoke. "No, no, no." The rocking boat knocked them backward in a heap.

Bird's anger broke. Her strength left, and she could not stop sob-bing, choking sobs that made it hard to breathe. Stoke girded her with his arms and held her fast for a long time. Slowly, the boat settled from its rocking and continued to float down the river, which was ever growing wider, deeper, and darker.

Eyes half closed, drowsy in Stoke's arms, Bird watched Dren doctoring Issie. Dren was washing Issie's wounded face with cloth torn from his shirt and dipped in the river. He called Finder and gave her to Issie to hold for comfort. For a time all that could be heard was the lapping of water against the boat's sides and Issie's soft whimpers. Bird was almost asleep when Dren said quietly, "Look at the size of those trees. And those ferns. We must be in the Great Forest of Wen."

Still wrapped in Stoke's arms, Bird opened her eyes. Tower-ing over her head were giant firs with trunks as big around as cottages. The riverbank was dense with fern curls, thick with glowing green moss. Here and there a stream splashed into the river, or a wind stirred a cloud of small blue flowers. Unmov-ing deer and rabbits watched the children voyaging on.

"Listen! Upstream!" Stoke cried.

Bird heard a drumbeat, faint but growing louder: *duh-boom, duh-boom, duh-boom*. "What's that?"

"Who knows? Something coming down the river. We better get to shore and hide," said Stoke.

Dren grabbed the pole to propel the boat toward shore. "I can't touch bottom."

Stoke held out the bow rope. "Issie! Bird! Grab this. We can swim and pull the boat." Clutching the rope, Bird, Issie, and Stoke jumped into the icy river. The swift current immediately seized Bird's sweater, dragging her into the river's depths. She could scarcely keep her head above water, much less help swim the boat to shore, but then she saw Stoke and Issie on their backs, kicking, so she turned over on her back too and kicked for all she was worth. Now at least she wasn't drowning.

Duh-boom, duh-boom, the beating sound grew louder, a giant heart pounding through the river, earth, and sky. In the boat above her, Bird could see Dren probing with his pole for the river bottom. Finally he shouted, "Got it!" and the boat shot forward past Bird and the others in the water. Dren poled for shore, towing them behind him.

When the children reached the riverbank, they pushed the boat as far as they could onto a gritty slice of beach. The sparse grass that grew there provided some concealment. They hid farther up the bank, behind some river brush. Bird crouched next to Issie, and even as the pounding boomed louder and louder, Issie said, her round blue eyes full of tears, "I'm sorry, Bird, I'm so sorry, I didn't mean for Ally to die. Please forgive me, please."

But Bird hardly noticed what Issie said, so horrified was she at the sight of Issie's face. It was hard to tell it even was a face. Issie's eyes were swollen purple-and-black lumps. On her cheek, there was an oval of small red holes, like stitches. "Issie. Your face."

"It's all right," said Issie, in a small voice. "I deserved it."

"No you didn't," Dren said, glaring at Bird with his sea green eyes.

"It's a ship," whispered Stoke. "Be quiet."

A huge ship had rounded the river bend, dozens of oars stroking from its sides. Round gold shields lined its railing, and scarlet soldiers with spikes bristling from their helmets stood at attention on its deck. Over all flew a flag emblazoned with the spider crest of Rendarren, gold on a field of black.

Alone on the ship's high bridge, a man in black stood hands on hips, his feet spread wide to steady himself. A curved gold sword hung from his belt and his long black hair flew wild in the wind. As he passed by, for a moment the man's eyes seemed to see through the brush and lock with Bird's. He grinned, as Bird had once seen a bully grin as he lifted a child by the hair and kicked him. The children stayed as still and silent as hunted animals until the galley rounded a bend and was gone and the drumbeats ceased to echo through the forest.

"That's him," said Stoke.

"He saw me," said Bird.

"For sure he saw our boat," said Dren. They all knew this must be true.

"I just thought of something terrible," said Issie. Her teeth were chattering so fast it was hard to understand her. "Now that Ally's gone he can't show us where the garden is. We can never plant the Seed."

"Your face!" exclaimed Stoke, and Bird felt greater shame than she ever had before.

"I've done all I can to doctor it," said Dren. "We don't have medicine. We don't even have food. Issie, how does your face feel?"

"The water was probably good for it," said Issie, shaking uncontrollably. "But what about finding the garden? I'm worried."

Stoke said, "We'll figure that out later. Right now we have to get you warm."

"Let's trade clothes," Dren said. He pulled off his sweater and tunic, the only dry ones among the children, since he had stayed in the boat. Issie ducked behind some bushes and changed. Bird and Stoke wrung the water from their wet clothes as best they could, as did Dren with Issie's wet castoffs.

"Are you up to walking, Issie?" asked Stoke. "Rendarren will come after us. We should hide in the forest if we can."

Now in Dren's dry clothing, Issie had ceased to shiver. But her eyes looked swollen shut. "I can travel, I'm sure I can. Who knows, maybe we'll find help. Farwender always came here, back to the Great Forest of Wen. There must be rebels somewhere near who'll take us in."

"But this time we'll be careful," said Dren. "Even an X on someone's hand doesn't mean a friend."

"I wish you wouldn't mention anything more about Nippy and Sebeelyo," said Issie. "I don't want to ever think about them again."

Soon the children were slowly trotting through the forest, headed away from the river, aiming to get as far from Rendarren as possible. The forest was clogged with fallen trees, rabbit holes, and bushes with thorns the size of kitchen knives, which made the going awkward. They went Stoke first, Dren helping Issie in the middle, Bird last. Bird imagined how silly they must look in Farwender's sweaters, striped and polka-dotted, starred and zigzagged, pink, red, blue, and yellow, like giant soggy butterflies. The soldiers would spot them in a minute.

The afternoon gave way to a chilled pink twilight, followed abruptly by night. There were too many things to run into and stumble over in the forest. They had to stop.

Running had kept them warm. After they stopped, all the children were soon shivering, even Issie in Dren's dry clothes. All they could think about was getting warm again, but they had left their steel and flint at Sebeelyo's, in their packs. They tried taking off their wet sweaters, but that was colder than wearing them. Bird, hoping somehow to make amends, insisted that Issie hold Finder.

They sat on the moss forest floor and chewed coils of baby fern fronds Dren had picked. "Try to pretend they're carrots," he said, but this was hard to do. As Bird chewed, the fern coils turned into a wad of tiny threads in her mouth. She spit them out. At least there was a brook nearby for water.

The moss that carpeted the ground felt like pieces of yarn, and Issie got the idea to pile it into beds. Working by feel in the darkness, quickly and desperately, each of them made a bed-sized mound and then burrowed inside it. It worked. Soon all of them were warm, even cozy. Issie insisted upon giving back Finder, and Bird accepted.

Overhead, the night sky was crowded with the ragged dark forms of great trees, stars tangled in their branches. Stoke said, "I know we're all tired, but there's something we need to talk about before we go to sleep. Soladin taught us not to go to sleep on a quarrel. I want to make sure that the air is clear between Bird and Issie."

"That fight wasn't one bit Issie's fault," said Dren, "at least what I saw. Bird attacked Issie, pure and simple. Issie didn't fight back at all."

"Bird did have a reason," said Stoke. "She was completely upset about Ally's death, which we all are. It's sort of understandable, from Bird's point of view."

"But Bird was so vicious, even though Issie never fought back. Bird acted like a wild animal," said Dren. "Issie will probably have scars on her face for the rest of her life."

"Bird? Issie? What do you think?" asked Stoke.

In the hours that had passed since the fight, Bird had become ever more deeply ashamed of her deed. She wanted fiercely to undo it, but it was too late. "I'm sorry, Issie. I know it doesn't take away the pain, but I'm sorry."

"I forgive you," said Issie. "Really, I do. And I'm sorry about going back for my dress. I shouldn't have."

"You're right," said Bird. "You shouldn't have. But I know you didn't mean for Ally to die."

"That's a good start," said Stoke, "but I think there's something else we'd better think about. It's that, well, Bird acted so terribly that I wonder if she should still wear the Locket."

Bird's hand went to the Locket, where it lay under her sweater. "Of course I should wear it. I'm the only one who can open it."

Dren said, "I was wondering the same thing. What she did to Issie was so ugly. Maybe it changed her inside so she can't open it anymore."

Bird's heart began to pound with fear that Dren was right. But she said, "That's stupid. Of course I can open it."

Stoke said, "You're probably right. But why don't you open it now, before we go to sleep, so we can all be sure."

Bird thought, If I try and fail, the others will know I am a fake. "Stoke just wants to wear the Locket himself," she said. "I don't have to prove anything to anybody."

"I'm with Bird," said Issie. "I'm sure she can still open it. When the Holder gives a person a gift, He doesn't take it away just because they make a mistake."

"What harm is there in opening it right now?" asked Stoke in his most reasonable grownup voice.

"It might give off a bright light," said Bird quickly. "The soldiers would see it and find us."

Dren said, "You're afraid to try."

"No," said Bird.

"Of course she isn't," said Issie.

"All right, enough," said Stoke. "We can talk about this in the morning. Bird and Issie are friends again. Let's go to sleep."

20

Another Feast

Day after day Soladin cried, not with great sobs, but with leaking tears of regret. Her tear-filled eyes gave wavy edges to everything she saw. They blurred the flames of candles into stars. Even as she slept, tears crept from her eyes, so that she woke with her face on a cold wet pillow. Yet the relief tears usually give never came, and her grief grew day by day, as if a grave were being dug inside her that could never be large enough for all she must bury.

—*A HISTORY OF WEN,* BY ISOGOLDE OF GILLADOOR

THE others went to sleep, but Bird stayed awake in her moss bed, listening to the wind whoosh long gusts through the looming trees. She planned to wait until she was sure the rest were asleep, and then try to open the Locket with no one watching. When the regular breathing of her friends assured her they were deep in their dreams, she pulled out the Locket, and held it a moment. She brought her finger close to the latch.

But what if she had lost her gift? What if the Locket stayed shut? It would be too terrible. In the morning the others would insist she open the Locket. If she couldn't, surely Stoke would demand she surrender it to him. And how hard it would be to look at Issie's purple swollen face day after day. What if the bite scarred and ruined forever Issie's golden beauty? Issie would probably still be kind to her, because Issie was usually kind to everybody, and that would make Bird feel even worse.

Bird tucked the Locket back underneath her tunic. She stroked Finder's warm silky back and considered the possibility of running away. She would go off by herself and look for Piper. When she rescued Piper, it would be such a good deed that it would wipe out hurting Issie, and she would be able to open the Locket again for certain. She would rescue Farwender and Soladin too, and somehow find the garden and plant the Tree That Speaks, all by herself. The other orphans would be mad when she ran away with the Locket, Stoke especially, since he wanted to wear it. But they would forgive her right away when she came back with a barrel full of thalasse.

Silently, Bird crawled from her moss bed. Finder seemed to want to stay sleeping, but Bird picked her up. If she couldn't have Ally, she could at least have Finder. Bird stood looking for a moment at Issie's swollen, sleeping face, shining grotesquely in the moonlight. Issie had stuck up for her against the boys. She loved Issie so much. An owl hooted, and clouds scuttled over the moon. Bird walked into the dark forest.

The ground was lumpy and pitted, and she kept stubbing her toes and walking into things. Finder kept struggling to get free of Bird's arms, so she held the cat extra tight. As she stumbled along, Bird made a plan: First she would find a village, then get food and a map. Then she would go to Sea Rim, the capital city of Wen, where Rendarren had his palace—and his dungeons. She would spy for information about captured children. But what if Piper had already been killed? Actually, there was a good chance of that. It had been a long time since Piper had been taken prisoner.

Suddenly, Bird fell headlong over a giant root. She lost her grip on Finder, and before she could grab her again, the cat scampered off, a small ghost disappearing into the darkness. Bird called to her, to no avail. Traitor cat, she thought. Go back to the others, back to your warm bed.

Cold, scratched up, and alone, Bird continued to feel her way through the forest. Weariness as heavy as sand poured into her. She would take a short nap, half sleeping and half listening for danger. She propped herself against one of the giant firs and closed her eyes.

SOMEONE grabbed Bird's ears and pulled her to her feet, dragging her from her dreams into life, into a night full of men and horses. "Stop it! Go away," Bird shouted, kicking at the big bodies all around. Then the horrid but familiar darkness descended upon her as a Searcher held her head in his hands. It was worse than she had remembered.

In her confusion and fear, Bird tried to cling to good and noble thoughts, as Farwender had once advised. She tried to think of Farwender himself: his bear paw hands, his amazing strength, his voice saying her name with enthusiasm and hope. But the darkness pushed those thoughts aside, like floodwaters carrying off twigs. When the darkness withdrew, she found herself in chains, riding horseback with a Searcher behind her.

At dawn, the Searchers delivered her to an army outpost. Soon she was in a coach, her hands chained, squished between two soldiers, bouncing fast over a rutted forest road. Three more soldiers were crowded onto the opposite bench. They smelled like bad breath and stale beer.

The soldiers talked loudly among themselves in a strange language, which sounded as if they were saying "Shush shush mush mush" over and over. When Bird asked where they were going, the soldiers made faces and laughed at her, but she didn't care. She knew they were taking her to Lord Rendarren. She tried not to think what Rendarren might do to her, but she felt as if a knife were already nicking her throat. She couldn't stop clenching her fists, hunching her shoulders. Would the Locket still protect her, despite what she had done to Issie?

After a time, the soldiers brought out lunch—bread, cheese, and ale. The smell of it made her stomach burble, for she hadn't eaten for over a day, unless you counted Dren's baby fern coils. She made her eyes big and orphanish and whined in her best begging style for something to eat. The soldiers made big eyes and whined back at her. They laughed and didn't give her any food, only a few sips of water.

On and on the coach flew. The setting sun flashed orange through the forest trees, and the soldiers napped. One of them tried to rest his head on her shoulder, but she heaved him away. The soldiers had been messy eaters, and while they slept, she ate all the bread crumbs and cheese bits within reach.

Then Bird slept too. She dreamed she was in a meadow of tall grasses and butterflies. Farwender was there, cooking breakfast over a fire. He greeted her with a wide smile and offered her a plate loaded with blueberry pancakes, bacon, and fried eggs the size of sunflowers. But when she reached for it, the food turned into teeth, which rattled on the plate.

When she woke, it was dark. The coach was slowing down. They were in a valley filled with army tents and campfires arranged as orderly as rows of vegetables in Soladin's garden. The coach pulled up before something that looked like a castle fashioned from silk. The castle tent poked into the air like a huge meringue pie and was lit from within to glowing magnificence. Hundreds of soldiers stood in ranks before it, their gold braid and buttons glittering in the torchlight, their banners bearing the golden spider of Lord Rendarren.

Everything Bird saw spoke of the power of Lord Rendarren. The Locket under her tunic, warm against her skin, seemed all too small a hope. As she watched through the dirty coach window, Lord Rendarren emerged from his tent. His black cape whipped back as he strode toward the coach, the soldiers parting ranks before him. He would probably have her tortured and killed. Probably the Locket wouldn't protect her. She stuck out her chin to look brave, as Stoke did when bad things happened, but she wanted to cry.

The soldiers who had been guarding her left the coach. Next, to Bird's surprise, Lord Rendarren climbed inside the coach and sat down beside her on the bench. It took her a minute to realize that the evil killer of the Tree That Speaks was actually unlocking her chains. He would have rubbed the soreness from her wrists, but she jerked her hands away.

He patted her knee and whispered, "Forgive me these chains, child. I thought I could not be sure of your coming without them. You have been told so many lies." He spoke in comforting fatherly tones, but she steeled herself against him, remembering his gift for making folk believe his lies. She would not be fooled like Soladin. She straightened her dirty rainbow sweater. Rendarren offered his hand to help her from the coach, and his arm for further escort, but she refused both. The tall lord smiled kindly. "So be it. Come along then."

She followed Lord Rendarren through the ranked soldiers and entered his castle tent, where the sudden brilliance of thousands of candles forced her to squint. Walking in the wake of his floating cape, she passed through chambers hung with draperies of red and gold, purple and black, blue and silver. She glimpsed beds piled with cushions, tables covered with maps, rooms splashing with fountains, cages full of birds, monkeys, and butterflies. For a moment they were enveloped in perfume as they walked through a garden of potted red roses. One room was thick with spiderwebs. Fuzzy, jewel-colored spiders the size of Bird's hand jumped from web to web.

Finally they came to a chamber more dazzlingly lit than all the rest, draped with gold and lined with mirrors. The high-domed silk ceiling was painted like a spring sky, light blue with puffy clouds. A long table in the middle of the room was heaped with a feast—meats, fruit, glossy sweets, great bowls of pudding, cheese wheels, loaves of bread, popovers, nuts, pies with braided tops. It smelled better than Soladin's kitchen, and Bird's hungry stomach cartwheeled.

Rendarren pulled out a cushioned velvet chair for her, then said, in a voice as richly lazy as a slow river on a golden afternoon, "So bless you, my little Bird. I have searched long and far to find you. I can scarce believe you are actually here, at my table. As you may have noticed, I have dismissed the servants. I wish to be alone with you." He flashed a debonair smile. He had lots of small white straight teeth. Oh snot, thought Bird. What is he up to?

"Does it seem too bright in here?" he asked. She stared at a fly crawling across a haunch of roasted pig. "Of course it is," he answered himself. He doused the candle flames with a golden snuffer until the light mellowed, then seated himself across the table on a throne whose back was a golden tree, branches, leaves, fruits and all. "How do you like my throne?" he asked.

She kept her eyes on the fly. It had stopped to drink some pig grease.

"This throne is the ancient royal seat of the Watchfolk," said Lord Rendarren. "I bring it with me everywhere I go. It's more comfortable than my other chairs."

Then there was silence. She looked up from the feasting fly to see what Rendarren was doing. He was staring at her. "Please forgive me for looking so long upon you, but you are a lovely child. You are the most beautiful child I have ever laid eyes upon. No wonder you are the chosen one, the one whose touch the Locket heeds."

He looked elegant and strong. He had high kingly cheekbones, a narrow jaw, and a beautiful white forehead banded with a thin circlet of gold. Against her will, she could see why Soladin might have fallen in love with him. She would never have admitted it to anyone, but Rendarren made Farwender look half finished, like the clumsy piecrusts she made compared with the perfect ones of Soladin's.

"If you're trying to win me with compliments, it won't work," she said. "I already know you lie about everything."

Rendarren smiled as graciously as if she had said "Thank you." He pulled his white napkin from its golden ring and spread it on his lap. "Let us dine. You must be famished. If you hunger for something you do not see, please tell me and I will have it prepared at once. And here, warm spiced wine, to celebrate." He poured steaming wine into her carved glass goblet, which was bigger than a cowbell.

Bird remained wary. Underneath the balm of Lord Rendarren's manner she felt something dangerous and cold, like a drawn sword. She reminded herself that he had ordered babies to their deaths. She must yield to him in nothing, not even eat his food, although her stomach clenched with desire for even a sip of water.

"I know you are afraid of me," said Lord Rendarren, helping himself to slices of pig haunch and mashed potatoes. "You've been told so many lies. But surely good food is good food, no matter whose table holds it. Do you fear I would poison you? Eat what I eat, then you can be sure it is safe." He carved a big bite of ham and popped it into his mouth. "Delicious."

Ah, she was hungry. All right then—she would eat; she might as well have a good meal before he tortured her. But she wouldn't drink the wine. It would never do to be tipsy when she most needed her wits. She made a mashed potato mountain on her plate and pushed a big chunk of butter into the center of it.

They ate without conversation, filling and refilling their plates. The food was rich and lively with strange spices. After a time, Bird felt the warm flush of relaxation that comes when a hungry person finally gets enough to eat. Stay on guard, she told her happy body, and then thinking a little wine couldn't hurt, took the smallest sip, to wash down the food.

Rendarren immediately replenished her wine. He held the flask high over her goblet, making a long, thin, red waterfall. "I would like to tell you my side of the story. All I ask is that you listen. If, when I finish, you wish to have no more to do with me, I shall not keep you."

Bird glared at him, refusing to answer. Then she helped herself to more chocolate puffpie. She doubted he would ever let her go, no matter how much she listened to his lies. She'd best eat as much as she could. Tomorrow he would probably starve her.

21

RENDARREN'S EXPLANATION

"Of course I trust you," I replied. "I trust you more than any-one in the whole world. And I love you. I think you are the most wonderful man that could ever be. Please, dear Rendarren, be-lieve me. But I cannot give you the Key."

—CONFESSIONS, BY SOLADIN LEAFSTAR, TREEKEEPER OF WEN

LORD Rendarren stretched back upon the cushions of his golden tree throne. He folded his long-fingered hands, knobby with rings, over his stomach. "First of all," he said, "I did kill the Tree, it is true, but it was a misdeed of my youth, and I am heartily sorry for it." His forehead wrinkled with earnestness and concern, as Farwender's did when he was sorry. "You know how it is—haven't you ever made a mistake?"

Bird thought of Issie's swollen bleeding face. "I know about mistakes. But you've done much more than kill a tree. You've killed thousands of people all over the world."

Lord Rendarren sighed, dropped his head, and then lifted it again. "I see that Soladin and Farwender have thoroughly poisoned you against me. Please believe me. My wars have all been self-defense. Kill or be killed. Such is the way of the world. I've tried to explain that to Soladin and Farwender. That's why I had them brought to me, so we could talk. But they won't listen."

Her heart ached at the sound of her friends' names. "Where are they?"

"All in good time. I'm coming to that."

She scowled at him.

He gave her a fond smile. "There's something important I need to tell you, the most important thing to me in all the wide world. It is the real reason I searched for you all these years." Their eyes met. She saw that although his body was slouched, his eyes were as alert as those of a man about to shoot an arrow. She felt a ping of fear. Then Lord Rendarren said, "I am your father."

Bird's lifelong hoping, waiting, and yearning for a father exploded within her. Fighting for breath, she grabbed her star blanket in her pocket and scrutinized Rendarren's face to see his bluff. He smiled at her adoringly, protectively—a father's smile.

"No!" she cried, jumping up from her chair and upsetting it backward. "I don't care what you say. You aren't my father. You can't make me believe you."

"Farwender knows I am your father," said Rendarren smoothly. "He didn't tell you because he feared it would upset his plans to regain the kingdom. He hid from you the one thing you wanted most to know in all the world: the name of your own father."

"If you are my father, prove it," she said, clutching her star blanket, still gasping for breath. She stayed standing. She felt safer on her feet.

"As you like," said Rendarren, still slouched in his throne, staring into her eyes. "For countless generations, a secret prophecy has been passed down in my family, that the Opener child would be of Watchfolk blood. There are only two who remain of our lineage—Farwender and myself. Has Farwender ever claimed to be your parent? No. That's because he isn't. But what do you care for genealogy. We have more visible proof." He motioned toward a mirrored wall. "Look at me. Look at you."

Determined not to believe him, Bird studied their side-by-side reflections in the mirrors that walled the dining chamber. Lord Rendarren had her eyes, black and slanted in a white face. He had her nose too, long and thin, and her long thin mouth. They looked as alike as a man and girl could.

The image of their matched faces pulled at her like the waters of a dark swift river. She feared she would yield despite herself. She felt there was something awful in the room, something she couldn't see, a vile mouth-thing that could suck out her soul, leaving her body a shell for spiders to live in. Rendarren smiled at her in the mirror.

"Liar!" Bird shouted. "My father is a good person. He fought in the wars against you!" For a moment she felt better. She could breathe again.

Lord Rendarren nodded slowly. "I know. It could be coincidence, our physical likeness. But I have more sure proof." He drew something from the inner breast pocket of his jerkin and unfolded it upon the table. It was a pure white cloth, thick with gold embroidery. "I think you know what this is."

Bird knew her star blanket as other children know their mothers' faces. She instantly saw that Lord Rendarren's cloth was her blanket's twin, each star and scroll and feather.

"Where did you get that?" she asked angrily.

"Your mother gave it to me so I would know you when I saw you," Rendarren murmured. "You see, she feared—accurately as it turned out—that we would become separated."

Her yearning for a father twisted inside her. How could Lord Rendarren possibly have this blanket unless he was her father? It had to be a fake. She sped around the table to his throne and laid her star blanket next to his. His blanket was much larger than hers, for much of hers had frayed away. And his was clean, while hers was mottled with rusty stains from the blood of Stoke's hand that Soladin had not been able to wash out. But despite these differences, Rendarren's blanket was without doubt the other half of her own.

Images of Stoke's fierce double-dark eyes and how he held his hurt hand against his chest burst into Bird's mind. She seized her blanket and stuffed it back into her pocket. "I don't care if you are my father. I won't be your daughter. I don't want a father who marks people!"

Lord Rendarren frowned. "Whatever are you talking about?"

"Two of my friends were marked, in Graynok, by your Searchers. Don't tell me you've never heard of marking."

Rendarren slowly shook his kingly head. "Marking. A gruesome custom. I have orders to punish anybody caught doing it, yet still it happens."

"Where did you take the children you carted off?" she asked. "That's what I want to know."

Lord Rendarren smoothed out the wrinkles in his star blanket. "Much has been done in my name that I don't approve of personally. Do I look the part of a fiend? Come, look into my eyes. See for yourself who I really am."

Wanting despite herself to somehow know if Lord Rendarren was her father, Bird slowly lifted her small black eyes to look into his large ones. Their eyes met, and she knew the truth.

"Yes," said Lord Rendarren, "you see it now. You must at least admit I am a handsome father. And you, my daughter, are as beautiful as sunlight on a garden. Here, take my hand. Such shiny black eyes."

His eyes seemed to trap hers. She couldn't look away, although she knew she must or something awful would happen. A blinding darkness flowed from his eyes into her body and her soul, and she felt ugly and exposed, as she had when the Searchers put their hands on her. He reached out his hand. Her small hand placed itself into his, as if she couldn't control it. He covered it with his other hand. If only she could look away. She stepped nervously backward, but when he said, "Come," she let him draw her toward him.

"I know I'm not the father you dreamed of, but I am your father," he said apologetically. "Breathe deeply now; relax. Listen for a moment. I'm not finished with my story."

She didn't want to listen. She wanted to run away and hide. His eyes were draining her, absorbing her. Again she fought for breath. Slowly, Lord Rendarren continued to draw her toward him until she was standing at his side. She had never seen anyone who looked more like a king.

"Although I am poor with words," he said in his lazy, golden voice, "let me paint you a picture. I am lord of all the earth. As my daughter, you will be the world's princess, heir to uncountable wealth. You will buy velvet gowns, pearls, ponies, chocolates, and sailing ships. Being the tenderhearted child you are, you will give away sacks of gold every day to poor children, until no one in the entire world suffers from hunger. Everyone everywhere will be happy because of you. Everyone will call you Dear Little Princess Bird. 'Dear Little Princess Bird has saved us,' they will say."

As Rendarren spoke, pictures of what he said came and went in Bird's mind like dreams. She saw herself looking delicately beautiful in Sebeelyo's pink gown. She was giving chocolates to ragged children, and then feeding a poor old woman soup with a silver spoon. Everywhere people adored her. They took her hand and wept with love.

Her mind was so full of dreams that she hardly noticed when Rendarren lifted her and sat her on his lap. He held her as a father holds a child he is about to tell a favorite story. With a rush of comfort, Bird realized this was what she had been yearning for all her life. The heaviness crushing her chest melted away, and her breath came sweetly easy.

Rendarren spoke on. "Everyone will love you. Princes and great warriors from many lands will swear devotion to you, writing poems and songs to your beauty and goodness. I too will love you. I will tell you so every morning and every night. I will hold you on my lap as now and tell you stories about kings and dragons and castles by the sea. But my dreams go beyond just you and me. It is the chief desire of my heart to at last undo all the wrong I have done. I wish to go—the two of us together—to the garden, to plant again the Tree That Speaks and thus bless my kingdom forever."

He placed his elegant arm around her shoulders and smiled

his father's smile again. "Give me the Seed, child," he said, "and I will be your father forever and ever."

Still held by Rendarren's eyes, floating in his blissful images, Bird tried to remember why she wasn't supposed to give the Locket away, even to a good person. She probably couldn't open it anymore anyway. Maybe Rendarren could open it. And now that she had a father, she wouldn't need the Seed, or the thalasse or the Holder or anything else. She would find Piper and let her be a princess too. Her father would set Farwender and Soladin free if she asked him, she was sure of it. She continued to gaze at Rendarren, to drink in his father's smile. Slowly, she pulled the Locket out. She took the chain in both her hands to slip it from her neck.

Suddenly, there was a thud and a crash of glass. Startled, Bird looked up. A white cat had pounced into the middle of the feast table.

"Finder!" Bird cried.

Finder snapped up a mouthful of trout, gulped it down, and snatched another. All of Soladin's training had never managed to keep Finder from gobbling fish whenever she sniffed it out.

Lord Rendarren sprang to his feet, spilling Bird to the floor. He drew his sword and hacked at Finder, who managed to jump away. The sword cleaved the fish and its platter, sending food and drink flying. Finder jumped into Bird's arms. Rendarren raised his sword. "Give me that cat!"

"No!" cried Bird. "You can't make me!" She tossed Finder as far away from Lord Rendarren as she could. "Run, Finder, run!" she shouted. To her great relief Finder fled, out and away.

Rendarren smashed some more food and plates with his sword. Finally, he wiped off his food-smeared blade on the tablecloth, sheathed it, and eased back into his throne. He smiled again his fatherly smile, and patted his lap. "Come now, where were we? Who cares about a cat? All that matters is I've found you."

"No," Bird shouted. "I won't give you the Locket. Never. Even if you are my father, which you aren't."

Rendarren, slouching in his throne, shrugged. "Then consider this, my daughter: Farwender has told you, no doubt, that the Locket protects you, and that anyone who takes it from you by force will die. But I've found a way around all that." He rang a golden bell, and soldiers came. "Search her," he instructed lazily. "Remove any weapons. Take off her boots. Remove her sweater and the white rag from her tunic pocket and burn them. I want her caged and starved to death. No food or water. Have the camp searched for a white cat and kill it."

Anger and shame washed Bird's mind clear. Even as the soldiers removed her boots, found and laughed at her scissor-blade knife, stripped off her rainbow sweater, and took her star blanket, she intently searched the room for what might be the Key That Sees. Her eyes systematically scanned the walls, furniture, and throne. There was nothing there that looked to be a curlicue of gold, as the orphans had described the Key. Then she studied Rendarren himself—the chains around his neck, his face. Finally she saw it. He wore it as an earring, and she hadn't even noticed. She had been so close she could have stolen it.

22

CAGED

"Yet there is one you hold dearer than I," Rendarren said quietly, and he flipped the Key, the twist of gold that ever hung about my neck.

"You know the ways of Wen," I said. "My love for the Holder kindles my love for you."

"But whom do you love the most?" he persisted.

—*CONFESSIONS*, BY SOLADIN LEAFSTAR, TREEKEEPER OF WEN

BIRD shivered in her thin tunic as soldiers marched her through the sleeping army camp. They came to the edge of a wood and proceeded along it. An outhouse stink reached her nostrils, and soon after, the soldiers' torches revealed cages, stacked three high. Dark forms, apparently people, hunkered in the cages, some moaning, others reaching their hands out through the bars, whining, "Mercy, a crust of bread, mercy." The soldiers ignored the prisoners and finally stopped at an empty bottom cage with its door hanging open. They pushed Bird inside, bolted and locked the door, and went away.

The cage was made of iron bars as big around as Bird's wrist. It was as long as she was tall, as wide as she could spread her arms. Despite her short stature, its ceiling was too low for her to stand. There was an empty metal bowl in one corner, some straw in another. The cold of the night plus the cold of the iron bar floor immediately penetrated her tunic and leggings. She quickly pushed the straw into a cushion between herself and the bars of the floor, but there wasn't enough. Soon her teeth chattered so wildly she bit her tongue, but she scarcely cared, so ashamed was she of almost giving the Locket to Rendarren. Only Finder's love for fish had saved her. It would serve her right if she froze to death.

The people in the other cages called out, wanting to know who she was and if she had food. "I don't have any food," she yelled. "Shut up." She scratched a fingernailful of frost from a cage bar.

A voice came, a gentle man's voice. "I am Benwin, in the cage beside you. Please, child, take this straw against the cold." Looking toward the voice, Bird made out in the neighboring cage the dark form of a man sitting hunched, reaching toward her with a handful of straw. She wondered how he would keep warm himself, but she didn't ask, in case he might take back his offer. Benwin gave her three big handfuls of straw. "Who are you, child," he asked, "and how do you come to be in this terrible place?"

"I am the orphan Bird of Graynok, and I made Lord Rendarren mad. He has sent me to starve to death in this cage," she told him. Benwin repeated this to those in nearby cages, who repeated it on, until word spread throughout the makeshift prison.

Benwin spoke again to her. "The Holder bless you, Bird of Graynok. You are only a child. At least the rest of us in these cages are grown."

"You asked the Holder to bless me. Are you of Wen?" she asked.

"Yes, and it is for my faith that I am in this cage, for Rendarren cannot bear to leave alive any who hope the Tree shall live again. Tomorrow I shall be hung. And you, little one, how is your faith?"

"I am also of Wen," she said. "I am the one everyone was waiting for. I opened the Locket, you know, with the Seed in it. But now I've done everything wrong and ended up here."

"So you are the Opener," said Benwin. "How strange and yet so good of the Holder that the Seed should be near me on the last night of my life. Rendarren would have let me go with a lashing if I had been willing to renounce my faith in the Holder and His Seed. Could you grant me a favor, child, and open the Locket, that I might see the light of the Seed before I die? Perhaps its light will convince the others of the truth of our faith, for we are the only ones here who believe, you and I."

Bird, bunched into a ball and shivering—for even with Benwin's straw she was cold—felt she might as well speak frankly. "I'm afraid I can't open the Locket anymore. You see . . ." And here she found herself telling Benwin the whole story, from the capture of Farwender and Soladin, to coming across the mountains with the other orphans, to Ally's death and her fight with Issie, to running away, to being captured herself.

Benwin listened with comforting aahs and hmmms. When she mentioned Farwender, Benwin said, "Ah yes, Farwender, of course." There was something so easy about talking to someone she couldn't see, a kind ear in the dark. Bird felt as if she were back in the cottage by the Rilla Nilla, talking to Farwender or Soladin. She even told the part about almost giving the Locket to Rendarren. The only part she left out was how Rendarren said he was her father. That had shocked her so deeply she couldn't bear to think about it, much less talk about it.

"I'll bet the Holder is furious at me by now," she said as she finished her tale. "That's probably why He stopped protecting me, and let me end up in this cage."

"Everyone fails, Bird," said Benwin. "I certainly have, many a time. Even Farwender has not done everything right. "

"I never saw Farwender make any mistakes."

"Farwender caused the Tree to die as much as Soladin did," said Benwin. "He was Watchman of Wen. It was his duty to watch over the Treekeeper, to see she kept a pure heart. He knew that Soladin refused to take the thalasse. He knew her mind was darkened, that she had separated herself from the Holder and our people, yet he did not stop her."

"Why didn't he?"

"He loved her. He knew if he told the elders about Soladin, they would banish her forever. He could not bear to lose her."

"Don't you hate Farwender?" she asked. "If he had done the right thing, the Tree That Speaks would still be alive. You wouldn't be about to die."

To Bird's surprise, Benwin chuckled. "Hardly. As I said, I've made mistakes too. It would be silly to be mad at other people for making them. Have you asked the Holder to forgive you for biting Issie? And for believing Rendarren's lies? If you wish, I will help you talk to Him. He will hear us."

"All right," said Bird.

Then Benwin began to talk to the Holder, as if the Holder were a real person right there. After a few moments, to her surprise, Bird felt a rush of peace and comfort. It was as when Far-wender gave her honeybread, or Soladin sang the sleep-well song, but better.

Bird pulled out the Locket and held it in her hand. She ran her finger over the engraving of the Tree on its surface. She wanted to comfort Benwin, as he had comforted her. She decided to try to open the Locket for him. Pushing back her fear, she touched her finger to its clasp. To her joy, the Locket opened as easily as the wings of a butterfly. The Seed spumed white sparks into the night, and all the prisoners oohed and aahed. "What is that?" they asked. "How are you able to cast stars into the night?"

"Ah, child! Such a gift! Thank you!" said Benwin. Then he raised his voice so all could hear: "It is the light of the Seed of the great Tree That Speaks, the promise of the Holder, who loves us all. Hear me, fellow prisoners! The first Tree is dead, killed by Rendarren who has imprisoned you. But soon the new Seed shall be planted, and another Tree shall grow in a day. Then the thalasse that is drawn from the Tree will heal and comfort us all."

"Enough of you," several prisoners cried. A woman's screech rose above all the rest. "Where is your Holder now, you fool. If there is a Holder, let Him open your cage!"

Then another woman's voice sounded nearby, low and husky. "Hush, Lilla. Even if Benwin's words are a child's story, we must let him tell it, for tomorrow he shall die for it."

The prisoners quieted. Sparks from the Seed continued to shower them all, as if someone had thrown handfuls of lighted dust among the cages. Then the display stopped, and all was silence and darkness again, with the exception of a glimmer in the Locket smaller than a grain of sand, which only Bird could see.

"Do it again," the screeching woman cried.

"I can't," Bird yelled. "Shut up. Go to sleep."

With some muttering here and there, the prisoners quieted again. Bird was amazed and grateful to know she could still open the Locket, but a question needled her mind. "Benwin? What about what that woman said, the screechy one," she said, whispering in case the woman should hear her. "Why doesn't the Holder set us free, you especially, since you seem to be so good?"

"Because in giving my life I do more for His cause than I ever could keeping it. I prove the value of the Holder and His way. That is my answer for myself."

"But I don't want to give my life for Him. And now I'm being starved to death, all because I'm wearing the Locket. I'm only a child. It isn't fair."

"Are you frightened, Bird?"

"No," she said. "Well actually, yes. I want the Holder to rescue me, not make me die."

"Here, take my hand." Benwin reached his hand through the bars. She grasped it with both her own hands and held it to her cheek. Benwin's hand was thin, cold, and dry, and on his palm she felt the crossing ridges of an X. They were both quiet for a while. She could hear the other prisoners snoring and the rushing of a river that must be close by.

"We don't know that you will die soon," Benwin said. "But when your time does come, just take the hand of the Holder as you are taking my hand right now, and He will give you the courage you need."

"What if I don't want to serve the Holder?" she asked, in a very small voice.

"If you don't serve Him, you will serve the darkness. It's one or the other. You don't want to help Rendarren and his kind, do you?"

"Well," she said, "I guess not. I just wish it were easier, serving the Holder."

"So do I," said Benwin, "but it isn't."

She fell asleep holding fast to Benwin's hand. When she woke, his hand was gone, and his cage was empty.

"Gone, child, hung at dawn," said the woman in the cage above.

23

The Key That Sees

Farwender lifted my limp body into his saddle, remounted, clasped me to him, and took off at a gallop. He shouted above the noise of the hoofbeats. "Yes, we are to blame, you and I and no one else. We have caused the death of the Tree and the end of Wen. We are of all people most to be despised."

—*CONFESSIONS,* BY SOLADIN LEAFSTAR, TREEKEEPER OF WEN

WHEN Bird heard that Benwin was dead, without thinking she reached into her pocket for the only constant source of comfort she had ever known, her star blanket. It was gone. Her almost broken heart broke completely. "Murderer, murderer," she screamed, as loudly as possible. The other prisoners yelled at her to shut up, but she didn't heed them. She yelled all morning long. She banged her fists against the cage bars, but that made hardly any noise, so she picked up the empty tin water bowl and clanged the bars with that.

The soldiers came at midday with food—bread smeared with grease. They gave none to Bird, but she, still clanging and screaming, didn't care. She was full enough from Rendarren's feast the night before, and the bread looked as appetizing as a raw frog.

By afternoon, Bird's anger was spent. She lay exhausted and shivering in the bottom of her cage. In her whelming sadness, she hadn't noticed that the fair day had turned foul, and that a cold wind bruised the sky with black-and-purple clouds. It began to rain, thick drops the size of pigeon eggs. The water glazed the cage bars, and Bird, thirsty from all her yelling and tears, licked the bars. Their rusty roughness scraped raw spots on her tongue.

Hunger, her old enemy, came to call. Now her mouth watered at the thought of the awful grease bread. She hated being hungry, the way her stomach squeezed in on itself, the way she could think of nothing but food. She imagined it would take a long time to starve to death. Once, as an orphan in Graynok, she had gone without food for five days, and although she had felt dizzy when she stood up fast, she'd never seemed at all close to dying. She searched through her two pockets for food that might have fallen into them at Rendarren's feast. She dug out a pea-sized crumb of macaroon, which she chewed between her front teeth. An instant of sweetness and it was gone.

She pulled out the Locket and opened it. The Seed light was the smallest it had ever been, barely a glint. She snapped the Locket shut and hid it back under her tunic. If the Seed light went out, she didn't want to see it.

What good was the Seed anyway, she thought. At best, it made pretty fireworks. It never gave real help. Ally was dead. Despite his brave words, Benwin was dead. Probably Farwender was dead now, and Soladin too. And Finder, fluffy Finder, had by now undoubtedly been found by some soldier and sliced to bits. And Stoke, Dren, and Issie. And Piper.

Night fell, a wet windy darkness. The soldiers came with

the grease bread again, and again gave none to her. Her nose was running. She ate the snot.

Why not give the Locket to Rendarren? What was the thalasse to her? She had survived fine so far without it. But she couldn't shake Benwin's words from her mind: "You don't want to help Rendarren and his kind, do you?" No. She would rather die than help Rendarren.

Was Rendarren really her father? His face floated in her mind, narrow and white as her own, and then images of his star blanket, fresh as the day it was made. Had he faked it all? Everybody said he was a wondrous liar. It could have been all lies and tricks, like those of the magician who came to the market each spring and pulled gold coins out of babies' ears and dragonflies from the noses of old ladies. If she ever somehow managed to plant the Seed, if she ever got some thalasse, maybe then at last she would know who her father really was.

Her sense of smell made keen by hunger, she drank in the odor of the rancid grease bread being devoured all around her. Her stomach cramped. At least she had rainwater to drink. She was afraid what it would be like, starving to death. Benwin had said, "When your time does come, just take the hand of the Holder as you are taking my hand right now, and He will give you the courage you need." But how did you do that?

"Holder, are you there?" she whispered. "I need help." She listened. There were only the other prisoners, gulping their water, gnawing their grease bread. There was only the rain, tapping the forest leaves, making everything wetter and colder. There was only the river, rushing free.

Outside her cage, a pine branch bobbed in the wind. Perhaps she could eat its tender tip. She reached for it, and as she did, she found she could stick her shoulder through the cage bars. The bars had apparently been spaced with the larger bodies of adults in mind, not the smaller bodies of child thieves, used to slipping in and out through cracks. After a bit of experimenting, she discovered that the only part of herself she couldn't get out of the cage was her head.

Well, she thought, I can hardly leave my head behind, although I might as well for all the good it's been. She sat for a time in the dark and felt glum and mad until it occurred to her that she had tried to squeeze her head through only one of the spaces between the bars. She might as well try them all; she had plenty of time. At about the tenth space, her head slipped through.

She quickly drew her head back into the cage and looked around for guards. None were in sight. But the other prisoners might cry out if they saw her escape. Her heart pattering fast, she made herself wait for what seemed like forever until she heard lots of snoring. Then fast as she could, she wiggled herself out of her prison.

She ran into the rainy wet forest behind the cages. It was so dark that right away she bumped slam-bam into a tree and fell backward, but she didn't care. She was free. As she rose and brushed off the muddy forest duff, she realized the mud was good camouflage. She rubbed it over the rest of herself and her clothes, until she practically disappeared right before her own eyes.

She heard footsteps. A soldier must be coming to check the

prisoners. She was only about ten steps into the forest. She held her breath and thought how stupid she had been not to pile her straw to look like a sleeping person. But then the soldier marched back the other way without sounding an alarm. He must not have bothered to stoop to check in the bottom cages. She would have at least until morning before they knew she was gone and began hunting her, maybe longer.

She would run for the river and follow it to a village where she could steal food and a coat. Maybe Finder would show up. She started stumbling toward the sound of the river, feeling in front of herself with her arms so she wouldn't bang into trees.

She had gone only a few steps when she remembered the Key That Sees. She saw it in her mind's eye, dangling from Rendarren's earlobe. Immediately she wished she hadn't thought of it, for her heart froze when she imagined going anywhere near Rendarren. What if he fooled her again with his lies and somehow made her give him the Locket?

If she could get the Key, she could find the garden. But how could she steal something Rendarren kept hooked in his ear? Well, she could sniff around, see the possibilities. She would be careful not to look into his eyes. Her feet were already walking in the direction of Rendarren's tent, even before her mind agreed. The Holder must be helping her. She would be a hero after all.

Staying within the forest, Bird edged around the army camp until at length she arrived where the trees came nearest the castle tent. The rain-lashed encampment was dark, and the castle tent glowed but feebly, as if everybody had gone to bed.

To reach the tent, she would have to dash across a cleared space, where she would be as visible as a bug on a bald man's head. To make matters worse, right in front of her were two guards, so close she could hear them talking.

"Has anyone caught that cat?" said one guard. "Rendarren's offering two hundred pieces of gold."

"Not that I've heard," said the other. "Wish I could be the lucky one. If I had all that gold, I'd leave this army. It's more dangerous than a war, being near the mad lord."

"Aye, true. He kills more of us than the enemy does. Any-time his dinner is cold he has someone's head."

"And then there's the executions of the thalasse folk. Even babies. I'm sick of it. Let Rendarren kill the next batch him-self." So it was true, Bird thought—Rendarren killed the folk he carted off. Had he killed them all?

"They say at times he raves that one of his own brats will bring him down in the end. The sooner the better, I say."

"You would think he would be more cautious about father-ing children. I've heard he's made hundreds."

"Or thousands. But he's killed them all. He's got a great mind for detail, whatever else you say about him." So she couldn't be his daughter. All his children were dead. Probably.

Then an idea came to Bird's mind like a bee to a flower. She let out a piteous wail that sounded like one of Finder's laments when Soladin scolded her. "Meeeeooooowrrr."

"The cat!" both the soldiers said at once, and plunged into the dripping forest.

"Meeoooowrrr!" Bird said again. Once the soldiers had

crashed past her, she sped across the open field and slipped under a tent flap.

She found herself in a kitchen, dimly lit by a night lantern.
It seemed as if all her best dreams had come true. She was
someplace dry and warm, and her nose sniffed the mingled
smells of a huge feast recently cooked. Somewhere in the tent
she could hear folk laughing and talking in a noisy drunken
way, but the sound was faint and far off. She decided the best
thing to do was to wait in the kitchen and have a nice dinner
until everyone went to bed, then look for the Key. She found
a long sharp knife and went to work on the ham and cheese,
one of her favorite food combinations. She hid under a table
to eat. She smiled to think that for the second night in a row,
Rendarren was treating her to a royal feast. So much for starving to death.

By the time she was pleasantly full and her pockets were
stuffed with raisins and nuts, the tent was silent. Holding the
knife in front of her—it had a blade as long as her forearm—
Bird slunk out of the kitchen. She made her way toward a far-
off snoring sound, hoping it belonged to Lord Rendarren. The
night lanterns gave only faint light, so she felt her way, sliding
one hand along the silken walls. With each step bringing her
closer to the snoring, her cocky smartness of the kitchen
melted away. All she could think of was the deadly pull of
Rendarren's dark eyes. Over and over under her breath, she
said, "Rendarren is a slugbrain," and that steadied her nerves
a bit.

As she crept nearer, the snoring grew thunderous and

snarly, and she began to fear that something not human made it—perhaps a giant. Then her hand felt a velvet curtain. The sound seemed to be coming from behind it. She took a deep breath and forced herself to peek in.

The odor of spilled wine and vomit hit her nostrils so strong she almost retched. In the dim light of a sputtering candle, she could see men and women sprawled over the table and floor. Many were snoring, with all sorts of weird whistles and gargles. It looked like the same feasting room where Rendarren had entertained her the night before, for there was the golden tree throne, and Lord Rendarren slumped in it.

Whoops! she thought. A crowd! She stepped back into the hall to reconsider. What if someone woke up? She stomped down her fears. If someone woke, she would hide under the table—or better yet, cleverly sneak away through the shadows. She had to get the Key.

Knife first, eyes and ears wide open with fear, Bird reentered the feasting chamber and tiptoed toward Rendarren. Her bare foot stepped into something cold and gooshy. She was afraid to see what it was. She tried to think it was cold mashed potatoes. She wiped her foot on the rug as best she could and continued more slowly toward the throne, now feeling with her toes first before she put down her whole foot.

Finally she came to Rendarren. His head lolled against the side of the throne, and his mouth was open wide as a stew pot. He was snoring with a big flapping noise. Which ear had the Key That Sees? She couldn't remember. He was lying on one ear. His long hair covered the other ear and any earring that might be on it. Ever so quietly, Bird laid her knife down on the table. Gingerly, she began to part the hair over his ear. All at once, Rendarren sat up and shook himself. She grabbed her knife and jumped back, prepared to run. But he laid his head down again, on the other side, with his hair fallen back. There was the Key That Sees, dangling from a hook through his left earlobe.

All she had to do now was pick it off his ear. She made herself wait until his snores were as loud and ugly as before. Then, holding her breath, she carefully pulled the hook out of his ear. There. She had it. She had thought her hand might tingle when she touched it, but it didn't. She dropped it in her pocket. She wanted to cry "Hooray!" and dance, but she made herself stay calm.

She gazed at the sleeping Rendarren. Was he really her father? Was she the one who would bring him down in the end, like the soldiers had said? She could easily kill him right now, driving her long thin knife through his temple with both hands. One of the other wildlings had bragged of killing a sleeping man just this way. But what if Rendarren screamed before he died and everybody woke up and captured her? It wasn't a practical time to kill him. And, truth to tell, even though she hated him, she just couldn't murder him. It would be too awful and strange.

Still, she wanted to do something so Rendarren would know she could have killed him. Working carefully with her knife, holding her breath lest she wake him, Bird sliced off a handful of Rendarren's hair. She put it in her pocket for luck.

Carefully, she returned to the kitchen, marveling at how easy it had been to steal the Key. Now the rain was worse. It gushed down on the tent like a river. Rummaging through the kitchen shelves, she found an oilcloth table covering to use as a raincoat. She cut a slit for a neck hole and slipped it over her head. The bottom dragged on the ground. She cut it off so she wouldn't trip. She was about finished trimming when lights and voices erupted in the passage outside the kitchen.

She dove through the tent flap into the drenching rain and sped across the open field toward the forest. She heard men shouting behind her, but she knew they couldn't catch her; she had too much of a head start. Then someone shouted right in front of her. She darted left, but suddenly—*crunch!*—somebody tackled her. The soldier expertly wrenched the knife from her hand and marched her back into the tent, straight to the feasting chamber.

The room was brilliant with light, packed with soldiers. Rendarren sat fully awake on his golden tree throne. Despite her desperate situation, Bird couldn't help but smirk when she saw how funny he looked with his new haircut.

One of the soldiers asked, "Is this what you were looking for, sire?" Bird's heart sank as she saw the soldier hold up the Key. It must have fallen from her pocket when she was tackled.

"Bring it to me!" roared Rendarren. The soldier with the Key obeyed, and Rendarren hung the magical object back on his ear. All her work for nothing. If only she hadn't stopped to make a raincoat.

Rendarren pointed at her. "Bring her here!" He sounded as if he wanted to kill her. Soldiers grabbed her and pushed her up to Rendarren's throne.

"Give me the Locket," he screamed.

"Never," she shouted back, looking up at the ceiling to make sure she didn't look in his eyes. "You can't make me!"

Rendarren leaped from his throne, seized her by the shoulders, shook her, and threw her to the floor. "Take her back to the cages. Chain her in. If she escapes again, I will have you all chopped to bits!" he yelled, and strode from the room.

The guards yanked Bird to her feet, removed her tablecloth raincoat, emptied her pockets of raisins and nuts, and marched her back to her cage, where they chained her ankle and wrist to the bars. The rain continued to pour from the night sky, streaming through the cages above her into her own. She was sopped to the skin. But she scarcely noticed how miserably cold she was because she was so angry at herself. She had been so stupid. She had had her fingers on the Key That Sees. If only she hadn't stopped to make a raincoat, she would be on her way to the Hidden Garden right now.

She thought about what the guards had said, about Rendarren's killing everyone who'd been touched with thalasse, even babies. Piper must be dead by now. She pulled Rendarren's hair out of her pocket and threw it out of the cage. She should have killed him when she had the chance.

24

THE BONFIRE

*My axe sliced easily into the Tree's soft, peach-colored flesh.
Each blow brought a new rain of purple blossoms until I stood
knee-deep in them. The blossoms' acrid odor coated the insides of
my nostrils until I retched from the stench. But I held to my task,
whacking out great chunks of wood with each swing. Much
sooner than I had dared hope, the Tree That Speaks fell.*

—*THE DEATH OF THE TREE,* BY LORD RENDARREN OF WEN

RENDARREN'S army struck camp at dawn and marched into
the Great Forest of Wen, bringing with it the prisoners in their
cages. Bird's cage was loaded onto a wagon all by itself and
given a guard of six horseback soldiers.

The rain had stopped, but the sky was lumpy with storm
clouds. As the wagon jolted through the dripping forest, Bird
shivered and dozed. Now and then her eyes opened to see
again the cage bars, the soldiers, the dreary green trees. She
had no idea where they were going and she didn't care. All she
could think about was how she could have been in the Hidden
Garden by now, planting the Seed, if only she hadn't stopped
to make a raincoat.

At least Rendarren seemed to have dropped his plan to
starve her to death. That morning, she had been given a cup
of water and a slice of the smelly grease bread. As before, she

had to do all her bodily functions in the cage, now under the vigilant watch of the soldiers. She relieved herself in one end of the cage and sat and slept curled in the other, trying to keep some cleanliness and dignity.

The day wore on to the drumbeat that set the pace for the foot soldiers. Bird floated in a stupor of anger, misery, and dreams, her senses shut down against the harshness of all that was happening. She closed her eyes and tried to comfort herself by remembering good and true things. She imagined herself again in Farwender's backsling as he ran through the night to heal Piper. She thought of Soladin, teaching her to braid her hair into a crown, and of Stoke, with his wounded hand, pledging himself as her brother. She pictured Piper, small and sweet, reaching up her arms and saying, "Hold you, hold you," because she didn't know yet she was supposed to say, "Hold me." Most of all, she remembered Ally's last battle, and how he gave his life to save her and her friends.

As long as she remained awake, she could fend off thoughts of Rendarren and his claim to be her father. But when she dozed, he rose in her dreams larger than life, crazy and ghoulish, and she woke panting, gripping the bars of the cage with both hands. Rendarren as a father was worse than no father. Someday, somehow, she would be touched with the thalasse, and the Holder would tell her who her real father was.

As twilight fell, she opened the Locket. The Seed light burned warmly orange, a tiny campfire. "Thank you, Holder, that the Seed light still burns," she whispered, "and that I haven't given the Locket to Rendarren." She tried to think of other things to be thankful for, but couldn't. So she sat and watched the Seed light, and as she watched, the swirling fears and hopes of her heart and mind gathered into one solid resolve: No matter what, even if she found out all the others she loved were dead, even if Rendarren starved her to death, she would not give him the Locket. No matter what, she would not help the darkness.

She slept peacefully then, but woke hungry and thirsty. A cup of water twice a day was not enough. She could think of little else than water. It rained again, hard, and she managed to drink several mouthfuls by wringing her drenched tunic into her mouth. This worked much better than licking the rusty cage bars and getting sores on her tongue. She was afraid the soldiers would stop her from drinking this way, but they ignored her. She noticed that one of the soldiers had a squashed-looking face; she named him Frog Face.

The army halted early, about mid-afternoon, and set up camp. Everyone seemed stirred up about something. Soon she heard the whack of axes, followed by the creaks and groans of breaking trunks. The ground shook as giant trees slammed to earth. What was Rendarren doing now? She tried not to care.

Hours later, the chopping ceased. She was just starting to relax in the quietness when soldiers opened her cage and grabbed her out of it. Roughly, they chained her wrists and ankles together and force-marched her in the direction of the logging noise. She hobbled along in the ankle chains as best she could, her arms grasped on both sides by soldiers. The fallen trees must have something to do with her.

They brought her to a clearing. Thousands of soldiers were laughing, eating roasted meat, and drinking freely from barrels of beer; she knew it was beer by the smell. In the center of the clearing stood a pile of logs the size of a barn, stuffed with heaps of brush. Soldiers with torches stood nearby. It looked as if they were going to have a gigantic bonfire.

The storm was over, and the sun was setting. The rosy rain-washed sky was strewn with shreds of golden clouds. Bird kept saying her promise to herself, that she wouldn't give the Locket to Rendarren. She looked around for Rendarren and saw instead a sight that made her breath catch: Farwender and Soladin were being hustled through the crowd by soldiers. They were far away. She could only see their backs. Soladin walked slumped, but Farwender moved with a little bounce. "Farwender!" Bird shouted. "Soladin!" Frog Face smacked her across the mouth.

Farwender and Soladin didn't look her way; they probably couldn't hear her over the noise. They disappeared into the celebrating soldiers. At least she knew they were alive.

A trumpet sounded, commanding silence.

From high above her head, someone shouted, "Hear, friends and true companions at arms." It was Rendarren. He was on the top of the log pile, his figure silhouetted against the pink evening sky, too far away for Bird to admire her haircutting job. The soldiers clapped and whistled.

He held up something too small for Bird to see. The setting sun caught it, making sharp points of light. "This, O comrades, is the Key That Sees, the famous Key of story and song, which opens the way to the Hidden Garden, where the famous Tree That Speaks once grew." More cheers.

"Soladin, the beautiful Treekeeper of Wen, gave this Key to

me. Using its power, I found the Hidden Garden and brought to earth the hated Tree That Speaks! That was a great day in the history of Wen!" The crowd gave a long cheer, with whistling, clapping, and stomping, which didn't stop until Rendarren motioned them to hush.

"Friends, today is another great day. From this day forward, we can all rest assured that no one will ever go into the Hidden Garden again. The Tree That Speaks will never grow again. We, and our children, and our children's children, will be safe from the enslavement of the Holder and his thalasse forever. Today we shall destroy the Key That Sees!"

The longest, loudest cheer yet followed. Bird was stunned. It had never occurred to her that Rendarren would destroy the Key. Now how would she find the garden? Rendarren threw the Key into the pile of logs, climbed to the ground, and gave the torchmen the signal to light the fire.

Flames leaped higher than the trees, while the whole army drank and danced. After a time, the soldiers returned Bird to her cage, where she sat and watched the long licks of light cast by the bonfire. The roar and crackling of the burning logs was louder even than the carousing of the soldiers. She had not given the Locket to Rendarren. He had not asked for it. He had found another way to ruin everything.

A night, a day, and then another night went by. Finally the fire burned itself out, but still the soldiers continued their revelries. For Bird, the time passed in a blur of grief. All the soldiers seemed to be drunk except the ones watching her. She wished they would get drunk too, so she might have a chance to escape.

Then one morning about a week after the fire, the soldiers again opened her cage and took her, shuffling in her chains, to the clearing, which was now a field of ash. Ever since her glimpse of them, she had been yearning to see Farwender and Soladin again, especially their faces. Now there they were, standing only a chimera leap away.

Bird's heart sank to see Soladin's pinched and fearful face. But there was something about Farwender, an aliveness, that gave her hope, even though he looked much thinner and older. Farwender cried, "My child!" at which a guard struck his head with a club and told him to shut up. Soladin turned away and buried her face in her hands.

Rendarren appeared, dressed in black silk and gold necklaces. He wore a baglike cap over one side of his head, to hide the place where Bird had cut off his hair. The rest of his hair hung long and glossy black. He pointed at Soladin. "Unchain her." When this was accomplished and Soladin was standing before him, he said, "Soladin, dear Soladin, I have a problem, and I wonder if you would mind helping. It's about the Key That Sees. How can we be sure it's destroyed? For all we know, it survived the flames, and lies at the bottom of this ash heap. So would you, dear, mind sifting through the ash for me? You can look all day, if you wish. If anyone can find it, I know you can." Then he sauntered off.

Bird wanted Soladin to look at her, so she could give her an encouraging smile. Then she planned to mouth the words "I love you," which she had never said to Soladin before. But Soladin only looked down. She kneeled and went to work, scooping and sifting. At first she wept as she toiled, but after a time she wept no more. Now and then, despite the guards, Bird and Farwender risked glances and quick, small smiles at each other, and once Bird mouthed, "I love you," to Farwender, and he mouthed it back. When twilight fell, Rendarren reappeared.

"Any luck?" he asked. He looked fresh, as if he had taken a nap and bath and changed his clothes. Soladin, covered with gray ash, her face a blank, said nothing. "Actually, I was sure it was gone," said Rendarren pleasantly. "I just wanted you to be sure. Chain her up. Back to the cages, one and all."

BIRD sat in her cage. She could hear the celebration getting rowdier, as it did every night. Off in the distance, some soldiers were blowing trumpets all out of tune. The soldiers drank at night and slept during the day. She wondered how long they were going to stay here, having their party. After a time, despite the noise, she fell asleep.

A familiar lazy voice woke her. "Daughter," said Rendarren, "here's a dear friend, come for a visit. Go ahead, brother."

Bird opened her eyes. It was still night. There in the torch-light stood Farwender, right by her cage, in chains, with guards all around. "Bird," he said softly, "are you all right?"

"Yes," she told him, "but Ally's dead." She had longed to tell him about Ally all day, as they stood watching Soladin, but she had been afraid that a soldier would hit her.

Farwender winced with grief. "I'm sorry," he said.

"Isn't it nice," said Rendarren, "how our sorrows grow lighter when shared with a friend?"

"And the others?" Farwender asked, but before Bird could

tell him, Rendarren interrupted. "Enough chat. Tell her why you're here."

Farwender said nothing. His face seemed full of love but also pain. Bird reached through the bars and managed for a moment to clutch the coarse cloth of his sleeve before Rendarren jerked Farwender out of her reach. Rendarren said, "Tell her. Tell her who her father is."

"Rendarren is your father," said Farwender in a low voice. "I should have told you earlier. I knew the moment you opened the Locket. I was waiting for the right time to tell you. But then . . ."

"Thank you, dear brother," said Rendarren. "Very nice. We'll talk some more later." He ordered the guards to take Farwender away.

"It's all right, Farwender," Bird called out after him. "It's all right you didn't tell me. I understand."

Rendarren leaned against Bird's cage. "Do you believe me now?" he murmured. "I am your father." Empty as her stomach was, Rendarren's rich voice made Bird think of butterscotch pudding. "And you are my little princess, the greatest treasure of my house."

The darkness of Rendarren's presence began to seep into her. She turned her back on him, to avoid his eyes. She scooted as far away as possible, scrunching herself into a ball in the cage corner.

"The same proud, noble blood runs in your veins as in my own," he continued softly. "And yet, if you do not relinquish the Locket, once we reach our ancestral home, I must have you confined to the dungeon."

When Rendarren said "dungeon," Bird suddenly felt as if she were already in one. She put her fingers in her ears, to blot out his voice, but still she could hear him. She shouted, "La, la, la, la, la," to drown him out, but still his soft words sounded in her head as clearly as ever.

"Would you like to know who your mother is?" he asked. "Give me the Locket, and I'll tell you her name. She had a very beautiful name. That Locket's worthless anyway, now that the Key is gone." He stuck his arms through the cage bars and began to stroke the back of her head. She batted his hand away.

"My mother's dead," she said. "Who cares what her name is. If the Locket is so worthless, why do you want it? Go away." She had often longed to know her mother's name, to say it now and then, but never at such a price.

"The dungeon it is then," Rendarren said quietly. "Nighty-night, sweetie." Then he left.

In the dark of her cage, with two soldiers guarding her, Bird considered all she had been told. Was Rendarren really her father? Yes, he was—Farwender had said so. Farwender never lied. Besides, there was the way Farwender had spoken, low and sad. It had to be true. She stared into the ancient forest. She felt creepy all over, as if teeny bugs were running up and down her body.

Not far away, some soldiers still celebrated. Someone was laughing, high and long, on and on. It sounded like Rendarren. Her father. Bird's father-wanting sadness crashed down on her like a giant falling tree. Her father was going to put her in his dungeon. She had dreamed of a father who would protect her and tell stories and love her. She had gotten a father who wanted to kill her.

She stretched out her hands into the dark. "Holder, are you there? Can you help me? I'm afraid of my father. I'm afraid my father is going to do something awful to me."

She listened and looked. There were only her two pale arms reaching out into the darkness. There were only the soldiers carousing. There were only the winter stars, shining ice dreams from the night sky.

She slept and dreamed in sword-sharp colors of a tall, whirling finger of wind. It gouged a path across the barren hills of Graynok, tearing up earth and grass, exploding houses, and throwing trees into the sky. It carved through the Great Forest of Wen, snatching up the largest trees as if they were saplings. It ripped through Rendarren's army camp, tossing tents, men, and horses. The soldiers tried to run away, but the whirlwind sucked them into its spinning belly. Bird watched the destruction from a grassy hollow, somehow knowing the whirlwind would not come near her, yet afraid nevertheless, because of its power. When she woke, her mind felt as clear as a blue sky after a storm, as if the whirlwind had torn away all her fears.

The army broke camp next morning and five days later reached Sea Rim, the capital city of Wen. Through the bars of her cage, Bird saw for the first time the fluted turrets of Seahold, the ancient home of her people, the Watchfolk, built on cliffs above the sea.

Soldiers locked her in a dungeon cell carved into the sea rock. Waves pounded against the outside wall. How long would they keep her here? At least the cell was bigger than the cage. She could stand up and walk. Through a window about the size of a human face, she could see the ocean, silvery quiet in the morning light.

Still she wore the Locket, entrusted to her care. She had done what could be done. She had not helped the darkness.

25

A Patch of Light

As I witnessed the Tree's death, power surged into my soul. For thousands of years my people had guarded and tended this Tree, believing it the sole source of the might and wealth of the kingdom, yet I had felled it in a matter of moments, all by myself. I felt as if I had grabbed lightning and hurled it at will.

—*THE DEATH OF THE TREE,* BY LORD RENDARREN OF WEN

THE boom of the waves echoing through her dungeon made Bird feel she lived deep inside a drum the ocean played. She spent most of her time burrowed in straw, trying to stay warm. Now and then, she rose to pace the cell—five steps, turn, three steps, turn, five steps, turn, three steps . . . Or she looked out the small window at seabirds swooping and fishing, at ships coming and going, at fog lifting and lowering.

Twice a day, a slot at the bottom of the door opened, and she pushed out her chamber pot and food bowl. Someone emptied the chamber pot, filled the food bowl with water and grease bread, then pushed both back inside. Once, along with grease bread, there were three mushy apples. She savored them as if they were chocolate.

Weeks passed. Her body wasted away until the bones of her wrists and hips stuck out sharp and her fingers looked like they belonged to a skeleton, not a living girl. Continually she thought and dreamed about food, especially ham and honey-bread.

In the afternoon, the sun would strike through the window, making a patch of sunlight on the rock floor of the cell. The patch would slowly move across the floor, rise up on the wall, and then, at sunset, turn orange, fade, and vanish. Bird loved this patch of sunlight. It warmed the rock where it fell. She would put her cold bare feet on the warm place, or press her hand or cheek against it so the heat could seep into her bones. Clouded days were so much harder than sunny ones, because the sun patch was gone.

Every day as darkness fell, her fears and sorrows crept from their hiding places and filled her with heaviness. She thought of her friends, especially Piper, until sometimes she wept. Often then she opened the Locket. The Seed light was never the same. One time it offered the quiet paleness of dawn. Another time it cast a light that trembled with leaf shadows. Once, it filled the cell with such brilliance that she had to close her eyes. It was as if she had looked directly at the sun.

It was strange to her to think that she was descended from the folk who had built this palace and its dungeons. She was home, in a manner of speaking.

She tracked the days by scratching marks near the door with the edge of her food bowl. At first she expected each day to be taken before Rendarren, who would try another way to make her give him the Locket. But as the days washed by, she began to suspect she would live the rest of her life in her cell, never again to see a human face.

ON the forty-first day of her imprisonment, a key clicked in the lock. Her cell door opened. She was watching six brown birds with white throats fly in a line over the sea, skimming a handbreadth from the water. She turned and froze. Four Searchers stood before her, black-robed and hooded. Silently, they chained her wrists. She calmed herself as best she could by fixing her eyes on the sun patch, which at that moment was high on the wall above the Searchers' heads. A Searcher clasped her head between his hands, and the darkness descended; as before, she went rigid, dumb, and blind. But she kept thinking about the sun patch, as if she could still see it. And she could still see it. It was there in her mind in the darkness, and as long as that was true, the darkness didn't bother her much. The Searcher grunted and let go of her head.

From the cell, they took her through a maze of hewn rock passages, up flight after flight of stairs, then into the fine parts of the palace. They proceeded down a long hall hung with tapestries of hunts and feasts, and then another hall hung with portraits of folk wearing crowns. Finally, they entered a great hall of polished gray stone that seemed big enough to hold the whole town of Graynok. Black banners emblazoned with the golden spider crest hung from rows upon rows of columns carved to look like the trees of the Great Forest of Wen. Hundreds of folk dressed in dark and gorgeous robes and dresses, adorned with glinting jewels, filled the place. This was the Great Hall of the Watchfolk, where for years beyond telling the ancestors of Farwender and Rendarren and Bird had bound their hearts to rule the folk of Wen, under the guidance of the Holder and the inspiration of thalasse. The magnificence made Bird feel as small and as powerless as a baby mouse.

The far side of the Great Hall opened to a vast view of the sky and sea, as from the heights of a cliff. Against this dizzying backdrop, on a platform above everyone's heads, sat Lord Rendarren on his golden tree throne. The setting orange sun spread its glory behind him. It was as if he had crowned himself with the sun, and when Bird looked at him, her eyes filled with sunspots.

The Searchers paraded Bird down a red carpet that ran like a long empty road straight to her father's throne. The soft carpet felt wonderful to her bare feet, which had felt nothing but rock for many days. She was dimly aware of the masses of fine folk murmuring as she passed by. Approaching Rendarren's throne, she heard the thunder of waves on the cliffs below. And then she saw her friends. They stood in a straggly line in front of Rendarren. Issie, Dren, and Stoke stood on one side and Farwender and Soladin on the other. Their hands were chained, but their feet free. The only ones missing were Piper and Finder.

Soladin's face crumpled with grief when she saw Bird, but Farwender grinned, as he always used to, his smile that said he was glad to see her. All of the orphans were dirty, ragged, and thin. None of them wore Farwender's sweaters. Dren's hair, which always poked up a bit in the back, no matter how much he wet it down, now poked out all over. He smiled at Bird and wiggled his ears. Issie's golden curls were greasy and matted, but her face had healed. Bird was too far away to see if the bite had left scars. Issie gave Bird a mild sweet smile. Stoke stood straight-backed as usual and kept his eyes fixed ahead, not looking at Bird. The look in his eyes, what she could see of it, appeared mad enough to pierce monsters. At this, her joy at seeing everyone drained away. Why wouldn't Stoke look at her? She wanted to say to him, "Don't worry, I can open the Locket," but fear of Rendarren held the words in her mouth.

Lord Rendarren lifted his scepter—a black rod with a gold spider on top of it—and the lords and ladies hushed, leaving only the boom of the waves.

Languidly, Rendarren pointed at Bird. He spoke in his lazy warm voice. "You. Give me the Locket. If you do, I'll let you and your friends go free. How's that for a generous offer?"

Bird studied Lord Rendarren's face. It was amazing how he could look so handsome and kind, yet be so deceitful and cruel. She was glad he wanted the Locket. That was all the more reason for her to keep it. "No," she said.

Lord Rendarren pointed his scepter at the Searcher nearest her. "You. Kill her."

Would the Locket protect her? At last she would find out. She held her breath. The Searcher who was supposed to kill her hesitated.

"You." Rendarren pointed at another Searcher. "Kill him." He pointed at the first Searcher. Immediately, the second Searcher strode to face his victim. He swung his blade around his head with both hands and—whack—sliced off the man's head. The head rolled to a stop at Bird's feet, still wearing its black hood. Horrified, Bird tried to move away from the head, but the Searcher behind her seized both her arms and stopped her. The assembled fine folk didn't even gasp. They were apparently used to bloodshed at great events.

"Now kill the girl," Rendarren ordered, settling back in his throne. The second Searcher, who was now standing right before Bird, at once lifted his sword. His black-clad presence loomed over her. Bird held her breath again and clenched her whole body. She hoped the Locket would protect her, but her eyes saw the naked sword and the severed head. Frantically, she looked about for someplace to run and saw only rank after rank of Searchers and soldiers ringed about her. Her eyes tracked the sharp curved sword as it flew backward and then toward her. Just before the blade touched her neck, it stopped. The Searcher fell down dead. All Bird felt was a whiff of sword wind. She couldn't help herself; she grinned at Lord Rendarren.

After a moment of shocked silence, the lords and ladies all talked at once. Someone behind Bird said, "Then it's true what they say."

"Silence!" Rendarren yelled. The Great Hall hushed. Bird snuck a glance at Stoke to see if maybe now he would smile at her. Still he kept his angry eyes straight ahead.

"I have an idea, a splendid idea," Lord Rendarren proclaimed. He pointed at Bird again. "Unchain her." Miraculously, Bird felt her hands go free. She shook her wrists, scratched her nose, and tried not to be afraid. What could he do? He couldn't kill her.

"Approach the throne," Rendarren ordered. She walked to the foot of the stairs that led up to the throne platform. There were about two dozen steps between herself and the evil lord.

"Listen to me, daughter," Rendarren said, in his laziest, most golden voice. "Give me that Locket or I kill your friends, one by one, starting with Farwender. He's the one you love best, isn't he? And the one I hate most. The children and Soladin will have to watch. Yes, that would be the most amusing way to do things." Rendarren pointed at yet another Searcher. "You—put your dagger to the throat of the old man over there and prepare to kill him when I say." Rendarren turned to Bird. "Now, daughter, give me the Locket and be quick about it." He held out a black-gloved hand.

Bird was staggered. She had not foreseen this. Did the Locket protect her friends too? She doubted it, and she wasn't about to find out by risking Farwender's life. The sun had set, and servants were lighting torches against the twilight. The silence deepened as everyone waited for her decision. Bird removed the Locket from her neck and examined its dull silver face, etched with the gnarled Tree That Speaks. It did not begin to look like a container for the world's greatest treasure. The engraved lines were worn away in places, from hundreds of years of Treekeepers wearing the Locket, keeping it safe.

She looked up at Rendarren. Obviously pleased with himself, he lounged to one side of his throne. She looked at Farwender. The Searcher had pulled Farwender's head back by his long gray hair, stretching his neck against the dagger's edge. With all the faith and fear in her heart, she cried within herself, "Holder, help!"

Then Farwender spoke, his voice strained and squeaky because of his stretched neck. "Brother, you know the prophecy. You cannot prevail in the end. The Tree will grow again. Why not turn to the Holder before it is too late, before your life ends?"

Lord Rendarren looked down his long nose. "There are many prophecies. I choose to believe a different version of events. And so far, you have to admit, my version would seem to be correct."

Soladin's feathery voice added, "Please, Rendarren. Even now you can turn to the Holder and know the thalasse with us again."

Rendarren shook a finger at Soladin. "You've been listening too much to Farwender, my dear. You fall under the sway of whatever man happens along, don't you? And neither of you seems to have a mind for details. I destroyed the Key That Sees right before your eyes. There is no way into the garden. You can't plant the Seed. You can't grow the Tree. You can't have thalasse ever again." Rendarren looked at Bird. "You have taken too long." He pointed his scepter at Farwender. "Kill him."

During all the talking, Bird had come up with a plan, plus a backup plan. Neither seemed likely to work, but she had to try.

"Wait!" she cried. "I'll give you the Locket!"

Rendarren raised his hand to stay Farwender's death. He smiled his kingly smile at Bird. She waited until the Searcher let go of Farwender's hair and sheathed his dagger. Then slowly, slowly, she walked up the stairs to Rendarren's throne, holding out the Locket in her hand.

"Bird! Stop!" Farwender commanded, in the voice of the great king he had been born to be. Bird obeyed him. Farwender said, "Don't give it to him. No matter what."

"I can't let you die," she said. "I just can't."

"You don't know that I will die," said Farwender softly. "Hold to your task."

So far, things were going exactly as Bird had hoped. Continuing with her plan, she looked at Farwender sadly, then turned and walked up the rest of the throne steps to Rendarren. Rendarren held out his black-gloved hand. Bird held out the Locket, but did not put it in his hand. She saw Rendarren's hand twitch, but he kept himself from grabbing the Locket. Oh, pig snot! she thought. Her plan had been for Rendarren to lose his patience at the last minute and grab the Locket. Then the Locket would kill him.

But she still had her backup plan. Instead of giving Rendarren the Locket, she climbed into his lap, clutching the Locket tightly in her hand all the while. Then she opened her hand again, so Rendarren could see the worn etching of the Tree.

"Enough of this foolishness," Rendarren said nastily. "Give me the Locket. Put it in my hand right now."

Bird gave Rendarren her smile that always made people think she was such a nice little girl who could be fully trusted. It was very like the smile Rendarren used for much the same purposes.

"Wipe that smile off your face," said Rendarren. Bird stopped smiling. Her backup plan was desperate but she couldn't think of what else to do. Rendarren locked his eyes on hers. "There's a good girl. Now give it to me." He leaned his face closer and closer to her, intent on bringing her under his will.

As he did this, Bird busied herself with the Locket, carefully weaving its chain through her fingers until it was thoroughly fastened to her hand. Then all at once, fast as a pickpocket, she grabbed both Rendarren's ears and, with all the anger and strength in her soul, she bit his long elegant nose. She tried to bite it right off. Rendarren's scream echoed all through the magnificent hall of the Watchfolk, filling the silence he had insisted upon. Fisherfolk far out at sea later claimed to have heard that scream. Rendarren's soldiers were so shocked at this sudden turn of events that they were struck as motionless as pillars.

Rendarren grabbed Bird's jaw and tried to pry her mouth open. But she kept her hands fastened to his ears and her teeth clamped on his nose, and had managed almost to bite it off before at last Rendarren got her mouth unclenched and shoved her away. She fell at his feet, on the step just below the throne.

Rendarren's face was covered with blood. He grabbed his long curved sword from the bearer who stood by his throne. Bird saw he was about to kill her. This had been her goal all along. But then Rendarren stopped himself. He pointed his sword at Farwender. "Kill him," he roared.

"No!" cried Bird. "I'll give you the Locket. I promise." She had managed to keep hold of the Locket through the whole nose-biting trick, thanks to winding its chain around her fingers.

Rendarren ignored her. His lust for blood controlled him now. If he couldn't have Bird's blood, he would have Farwender's.

But before the soldier could slit Farwender's throat, there was another scream in the Great Hall, a scream even more horrible than the one Rendarren had let out when Bird bit his nose. The fisherfolk far out at sea heard this scream too; it blasted so loudly they had to plug their ears. It was Soladin, howling the battle cry that Wenish warriors give to curdle the blood of their foes. All who heard it felt as if a bottomless black pit had suddenly opened underneath their feet and they had fallen into it. While everyone was frozen stiff with fear, Soladin rushed at Rendarren, right up the throne steps. Her honey-silver hair flowed down to her waist, as thickly tangled as the forest of Wen. As she neared Rendarren, she raised her bound hands high above her head, and Bird saw a flash of silver. Did Soladin have a dagger?

Searchers started forward to grab her.

"Leave her alone," shouted Rendarren. "This pleasure is mine."

Soladin stopped just before she reached the throne. Her way was blocked by Bird, who still lay on the top step where Rendarren had thrown her. All eyes were on Soladin and her suicidal attempt to save Farwender's life—or whatever it was she thought she was doing. Desperately, Bird worked to free the Locket chain from her fingers. Then she slipped the Locket into Soladin's boot. At almost the same time, Soladin lunged for Rendarren, to drive her dagger into his gold-chained chest. He jumped aside, and she fell headlong across the throne platform. As she madly tried to scramble to her feet, Rendarren gripped his long curved sword with both hands, as if it were an axe, and chopped down toward her neck. But the sword never touched Soladin. It jerked to a stop just short of its target, and Lord Rendarren fell dead with a thud. The Locket in Soladin's boot had done its work.

Everyone in the Great Hall rushed toward Rendarren's throne to see what had happened. Soldiers and Searchers pressed the crowd back. Someone yelled, "There's not a mark on him! What killed him?"

Soladin rose to her feet, lifted her face to the ceiling, and wept. Bird heard a clink. It was Soladin's dagger, fallen to the floor. Bird picked it up and saw that the dagger was actually half of the scissors. She stuck it in her pocket.

In the confusion, Bird thought there might be a chance for escape. Leaving the Locket in Soladin's boot in case the soldiers tried to kill the Treekeeper, crawling to escape the notice of the soldiers swarming the throne platform, Bird managed to get down the steps to Farwender. She recognized him by his red-and-yellow-striped socks, and stood up beside him. He whispered to her, "You gave Soladin the Locket, didn't you. Good work. And wasn't Soladin magnificent. This is turning out far better than I'd ever imagined."

"But what's going to happen now?" asked Bird. "How do we get out of here?"

26

THE REBELS

Dearest Mama,

The babe is born, a little girl. I am taking her into hiding, for I am sure Rendarren will kill her, as he murders all born of his loins. The birth was hard, and I am sick unto death. I pray only to live long enough to find a mother for my child. I have cut her swaddling blanket in two and send this half to you, for it is my fancy that somehow somewhere you will find her, and know her for your own. A childish fancy, but it is all I have. I have named her after you.

Your loving daughter,
Elara of Sea Rim

ONE of the soldiers grabbed Bird's arm. It was her old jailer, Frog Face. She struggled to wriggle away. Frog Face smacked his lips and gripped her harder. Around her, Bird saw that Farwender and the others also were seized. Bird's heart sank. It didn't seem to matter that Rendarren was dead—they were going to spend their lives in prison anyway. The soldiers, quick as ants on a hot rock, pushed Bird and her friends through the anxious, noisy crowd. Frog Face had forgotten to rechain her hands, but Bird couldn't figure out how to take advantage of this. It seemed she had used up all her good ideas to kill Rendarren.

The soldiers marched them double-time along a gallery with windows open to the sea, then down many flights of stairs, which became ever more narrow, steep, and dark. Why did they have to go so fast? For a moment, Bird wished she had taken the Locket back from Soladin, for perhaps they were being marched to their deaths. Their captors pushed them through a low door and then, suddenly, they found themselves outside, on a seawall. A full moon blessed the black sea and night. A long narrow boat with a single mast was moored close by. "Fooled you, didn't I?" said Frog Face in Bird's ear. "You've been rescued! Now hush and haste, into the boat."

"Thank you, thank you," Bird whispered to Frog Face. All around her, soldiers were undoing chains. After many quick hugs and quiet hoorays, and everybody saying how frightened they had been and how they couldn't believe they had escaped, they all piled into the boat—a fishing boat, from the smell of it. Some soldiers rowed while others hoisted the sail. Soon they were flying into the night under a stiff wind, tacking out to sea. Dren and Stoke shared the front bench, with Issie and Bird behind them. Then came Farwender, with his arms wrapped around Soladin, her head lying against his chest. Seven or so soldiers sat in back, working the sail and the tiller.

"Many thanks, Skoon," said Farwender (for Skoon turned out to be Frog Face's real name). "I'm sure we would all be headed for the dungeons now if it were not for your fast thinking."

"We were ready and hoping for the chance, sire. And there it was, like a miracle. The Holder still makes a way for His own."

The wind blew cold. Bird sat silently, stunned by their escape and the death of her father. The soldiers pulled blankets from a chest, enough for everyone to wrap up warmly. They gave out chunks of fresh bread spread with creamy cheese and passed around a jug of apple drink. Skoon explained they were headed for a rebel camp, hidden on the rocky northern shore.

"You were so brave," said Issie to Bird. "If it weren't for you, we'd all be dead."

The moon silvered stitchlike scars high on Issie's cheek where Bird's teeth had broken her skin. Bird wished for the thousandth time that she had held her temper.

Issie said, "Soladin and I were in a cell together. I gave her the scissors. I thought we were going to be in that dungeon forever."

"So did I," said Dren. "Stoke and me were together too. We had beetle races. Stoke's beetle usually won." He took another big bite of bread.

Bird looked at Stoke. The moonlight cast deep shadows on his face, making him appear more a man than a boy. She heard Farwender murmur to Soladin, "Rest now, dearest. Sleep. You did it, my love. It was your fierceness saved the day. Now all is well."

"How are you, Stoke?" asked Bird quietly.

"Fine," said Stoke, in a flat voice that told Bird no more than she knew before.

"So, Skoon," said Farwender, "what would you advise we do next?"

Then began a long discussion about men, horses, weapons, and strongholds. The trouble, according to Skoon, was that without the thalasse they might lack the courage and strength they would need to oust Rendarren's successors. The rebels, although well organized, were outnumbered and poorly armed.

But on the other hand, there was no logical successor to Rendarren's throne. He had kept as much power as possible to himself, so most likely his generals would fight over his empire. The whole thing might fall of its own weight. Perhaps the thing to do was stand back and wait until the generals had killed each other off as much as possible. Then Farwender and the rebel army could step in and take over.

Looking back toward shore, Bird watched the blazing lights of Seahold grow more distant, and then disappear. The soldiers turned the boat northward. Bird kept thinking about Piper. Where was she tonight? Finally, Bird broke into the discussion of swords and strongholds to ask, "Skoon, do you have any news of the ones that were carted off? The folk who'd had thalasse?"

An awful silence filled the boat. Finally Skoon spoke. "Most of those taken were put to the sword. The best that can be said is it was a swift death. We managed to rescue only a handful. Thousands were slain."

Bird remembered Piper's small arms reaching out to her as she said, "Hold you, hold you."

"Were any children rescued?" she asked. "Is there a small girl named Piper? She's very friendly. That's the first thing people notice about her. And she has big blue eyes. And long eyelashes like star points."

"Some children were saved," said Skoon, carefully. "There may be some in the camp we're headed for. We hope someday to return them to their parents. But I must warn you, I'm sorry to say, that it's unlikely your little friend survived. Rendarren usually had the children killed first."

"Which is why we must fight!" said a young soldier. "Surely the Holder will give us victory against such evil." And the talk returned to battles.

Bird stared at the waves peeling off the boat prow. The round moon laid its silver path upon the ruffled sea, seeming to promise someplace wonderful just beyond sight. But Piper was probably dead, and the Hidden Garden was lost to them forever. Bird would never know the thalasse, Stoke no longer seemed to be her friend, and—although he had been an evil man—her father was dead. Despite the sweetness of victory, Bird sorrowed for the way life was, for the way that dreams did not always come true.

She felt a hand cover her own and looked up to see Soladin. "I have grieved for you these many days," said the Treekeeper in her feathery voice. "I had thought I would never see your face again, yet here you are, and you have saved my life. Do not grieve for Piper before you must." Then Soladin gave the Locket back to Bird.

DEEP in the night, they reached the rebel camp. Everyone roused at once to see Farwender and the girl who could open the Locket. The rebels were keen to hear the story of Rendarren's death and to discuss what to do next. They gathered in a clearing in the Great Forest, about a hundred folk, mostly men. Fearing discovery, they lit no fire, but the full moon gave good light. Scanning the crowd, Bird did not see Piper. There were no small children at all. Perhaps the littlest ones had been left in bed asleep, she thought. She pressed through the throng around Farwender and touched his arm. "Bird?" he said, in a way that told her she was dear to him.

"Would you help me find Piper?"

"Patience. First we must give our good news, which these friends have waited many years to hear. When we finish, I will help you search." Bird waited, impatiently.

The rebels had Farwender tell them, twice over, the story of Rendarren's death. They cheered when Farwender related how Bird climbed into Rendarren's lap and bit his nose, and how she put the Locket in Soladin's boot. Bird scarcely heard the cheers. She could think only of Piper and her blue star eyes.

Everyone wanted to see the Seed, so Bird opened the Locket. At once the moonlight vanished, and for a few moments, the meadow was bathed with slanted golden light, as if it were suddenly afternoon. Everybody gasped; some wept. Someone shouted, "Let's plant it now! To the garden!" Farwender waited until all hushed. Then he told them that the Key That Sees was gone forever. The crowd muttered and grumbled.

"But we must trust the Holder," said Farwender gently, looking from person to person, as if to give each one the faith of his own heart. "Even though it seems unlikely now, someday we will plant the Seed in the Hidden Garden. This has been foretold before the time of story and song."

Quietly, gravely, the rebels laid plans to ride against Rendarren's forces, to take back the land of Wen. Farwender went off into the crowd, and Bird pushed her way after him. When she caught up with him, he was talking to an older woman, plain and square-faced, thickly wrapped in shawls.

"This is Mara," Farwender said. "She tends the children who were rescued."

Mara listened to Bird's description of Piper. She took Bird's hand in her own and patted it. "Could be, could be," she murmured.

Bird swallowed hard and began to hope. "So you have seen her?"

Again Mara said, "Could be." She bid Bird follow her.

The air smelled of pine and sea. As they walked through the mammoth trees, Bird saw everywhere tents made of branches and canvas. Mara stopped at a lean-to hardly big enough for a goat. She pulled aside a canvas curtain, revealing six or seven small children cocooned in blankets, lying every which way. Some squirmed as the moonlight touched their faces.

Immediately Bird saw Piper. The little girl was near the back of the tent, curled on one side, her dark lashes long on her cheeks. And there in her arms was the white cat Finder. Truth to tell, to discover Piper and Finder together and safe was more of a wonder to Bird than opening the Locket, or the death of Rendarren, or being rescued by Skoon and his men. In later years, when she would tell her story, Bird would always say, "And finding Piper alive and well, with Finder in her arms, was as the thalasse to me—a great strengthening of my heart."

27

The War

During our exile, I often told Farwender that I would willingly give my life if I could just once spit into Rendarren's handsome face. Farwender, however, reminded me that Rendarren was his brother and continued to pray for him. Sometimes I wondered if Farwender had experienced the thalasse too deeply to be of any worldly good. Perhaps his brain had grown soft as well as his heart. But then I would see him practicing his sword work and take heart.

—*CONFESSIONS*, BY SOLADIN LEAFSTAR, TREEKEEPER OF WEN

THE rebel camp rose before dawn to shoe horses, mend armor, and sharpen swords. Soladin, gaunt and pale, her hair again tidy in its crown of braids, helped organize and pack supplies. "Men should not have to fight on empty stomachs," she kept saying as she ordered Issie and Bird this way and that, collecting, counting, boxing.

Piper and Finder trailed Bird everywhere, which Bird loved, for she could constantly see that she was not dreaming, that both still lived.

Piper was almost three now, but small for her age. The little girl chattered ceaselessly. She seemed to remember Bird, even though she had been so young when they parted. She could say Bird's name correctly now. Every minute or so, Piper called, "Bird? See how far I can jump?" "Bird? Can I have a drink?" "Bird? Let's pretend we're sea otters."

Stoke ignored Bird. He and Dren were both to go with Farwender, not as warriors, but as aides. Still, they were to have swords, smaller versions of the huge two-handed weapon Wenish soldiers carried crosswise on their backs. Bird wanted to go with them, but Soladin would have none of it, nor would she let Bird have a sword or even a dagger. "You've never learned to use them. We need all the weapons we have in the hands of people who know what to do with them. There will be plenty to do in this war besides killing people." So Bird hid her scissors half in the top of her new boots and tried to be content, like Issie.

Everywhere Bird went, folk seemed to almost worship her. Even gray-bearded men looked at the ground when they spoke to her. They called her Milady Bird and sometimes dropped to one knee. Bird tried to explain that her exploits were all the Holder's doing, that He had given her the good ideas she needed to bring about Rendarren's death. This only made folk marvel at her humbleness.

Bird overheard a mother say, as she scolded her child, "Now Husk, behave yourself. Be good like Bird." Bird laughed to herself, thinking how that mother might feel if Husk started biting people.

She was glad nobody seemed to know that Rendarren was her father. She felt strange and confused about helping kill her own father, even though he had been so horrible. She tried not to think about it. When by accident she did think about it, she picked up Piper and held her close until she felt like a good person again.

FOUR days later, the rebel warriors were ready to ride to Sea Rim. They would travel at night, by the light of the almost full moon. At Sea Rim, they would face what remained of Rendarren's army, which had, as Skoon predicted, already killed off part of itself in battles over who should be in charge. Deserters from Rendarren's army were already trickling into the rebel camp, and news had come of folk from conquered lands riding to rally under Farwender's banner, the Chimera Rampant.

As the army's last day in camp wore on, Bird watched for a chance to talk to Stoke. She wanted to find out why he was being so odd and cold. But every time she came near him, he walked quickly away, as if on important business.

Dusk found Bird helping Mara take Piper and the other rescued children to the lean-to for bed. Piper was riding Bird piggyback, and the other children were marching, pretending to be soldiers. Finder kept her distance, hiding behind ferns, scrambling up and down trees. Finder didn't like to appear to be part of a group.

Suddenly on the path in front of Bird, Stoke appeared. He dropped to one knee. She could see the hilt of his new sword sticking up over his left shoulder. "I need to talk to you," he said.

"I'll take care of the little ones," Mara told Bird. She took Piper from Bird's back, hushing her yowls, and shooed the children onward.

When they were alone, Stoke said grimly, "We ride tonight."

"I know," said Bird. "Soladin won't let me go."

"I might die."

"Probably not. Farwender promised Soladin you wouldn't be anywhere near real fighting. Why are you kneeling? Stop it. It makes me feel funny."

Stoke rose, frowning. He took a deep breath. "What I wanted to say is I think you were brave, there with Rendarren," he said stiffly. Bird wasn't sure, but she thought he sounded mad. "I've never seen anybody so brave," he continued. "You are the right one to wear the Locket. Before, I always thought I should wear it."

"Thanks," said Bird. She was glad he thought she was brave. But was he still her friend? Was he still her brother? He seemed not to like her anymore.

Stoke dug inside the leather soldier's bag slung from his shoulder. "And I wanted to give this back." He held out the crystal thalasse vial.

"You keep it. I don't need it."

"You might someday, when you plant the Tree. If I die in battle, it might fall into enemy hands."

"It's hard to see how we will ever plant the Seed," said Bird, but she took the vial.

Quickly, awkwardly, Stoke bowed. "This is good-bye. I won't see you for a long time, maybe never."

"Why are you acting like this?" Bird burst out. "What's wrong? I'm your sister, remember? Are you still my brother?"

Stoke looked at her with his raw, true gaze that Bird loved.

She stared back, and saw the beginning of the man he was be-coming, a man with a warrior's heart and the strength to do right though it cost him all.

He said, "I failed you. It's hard for me to tell you that. I will always be your brother."

A battle horn sounded to call the warriors to ride. Words thrust up inside Bird, words she knew she must say now, in case she never had another chance. "Stoke," she blurted out. "I love you."

The battle horn rang louder, yet Stoke lingered, looking at her. Finally he said, "I love you too." Then he leaned forward and kissed her lightly on the forehead.

A few moments later, Bird watched the men ride to war. Stoke held her eyes with his own as he passed by. She spent the afternoon walking by the sea, letting the waves wash and gentle the rage of love and worry in her heart.

28

SOLADIN'S GARDEN

I wish to thee a joyous tickle,
A touch of love
And wonder.

—*FOREST SONGS,* BY LONGSTILL, WATCHMAN OF WEN

IN the space of a year, Farwender sat again as Watchman upon the golden tree throne at Seahold. Rendarren's army had been pushed back well beyond the borders of Wen, but the war did not end. Bands of Searchers roamed in far-off places, ravaging and ruining like a pestilence. Farwender's troops hunted them, with little success. The war, said Farwender, was like a wound that would not heal.

In Farwender's side was another wound that would not heal. During a battle, he had suffered a deep cut upon the scar of a wound Rendarren had inflicted on him the night the Tree died. The wound festered, sapping the Watchman's strength.

Despite his wound and the unfinished war, Farwender kept hope in the Seed. He still believed that someday, somehow, they would again find the Hidden Garden. Soladin pursed her lips and looked out the window when he spoke of this, for she thought it quite unlikely. "At least," she said, "the death of Rendarren is as the thalasse to me."

Farwender and Soladin married, and Farwender said to his bride, after their vows, "Your love is as the thalasse to me." Soladin answered, "And yours, lord, to me."

Soladin and Farwender hoped someday to have children of their own, but that did not stop them from adopting the four orphans. Bird told Farwender, "You are the father I always wanted." Yet sometimes in the twilight, as she watched the light leave the sea, her father-wanting returned, a slow, dark weight upon her heart. Then she would run to find Farwender. She never told him her feeling. She would just sit with him, knitting or playing cards.

"At least some good has come from Rendarren's life," Farwender said to Bird one night as they cracked and ate walnuts before the fire. "At least there's you. I have to admit, I'm curious about who your mother was. But I suppose we'll never know." Bird wondered the same thing.

The other orphans lived away from Seahold. Stoke had never returned from the wars, but had become a soldier, and fought on in far-off lands against the Searchers. He wrote Bird often, and she him, and the love between them grew.

Dren was apprenticed in a nearby village to a master carver of wood and stone. Issie lived four or five days away by horseback. She was a helper at a quiet house, where those in need of healing went. She was learning to be an Imparter, one who spoke the ancient stories, which were thought to contain some of the power of the lost thalasse. Farwender had an Imparter come to him each day and would not speak or eat until he heard a story.

As the Opener and only heir of the Watchfolk, the royal

house of Wen, Bird was named to someday sit upon the golden tree throne. So she stayed on at Seahold to learn to rule.

No Treekeeper was appointed to serve after Soladin. "If the Tree should grow again, it will choose its own keeper," she said.

RIGHT after Bird found Piper, she had sent a message to Twist to tell her Piper was alive and well. When it was safe to travel, in the summer two years later, Bird and Piper journeyed over the Pokadoon Mountains to Graynok, so Piper might be reunited with her mother. Piper had just celebrated her fifth birthday, and Bird was fourteen or fifteen. Piper scarcely remembered Twist. Indeed, she thought of Bird as her mother.

Twist had married an olive farmer, and lived comfortably in the again thriving hamlet of Graynok. She received Piper as if the child had returned from the grave.

"I have been a terrible friend to you," said Twist to Bird. "I betrayed your friends, and yet you have been so kind to me. If there is ever anything I can do for you, please tell me."

"There is one thing," said Bird, smiling though her heart was heavy. "Let me come each year to see Piper." And so it was agreed.

Twist asked, "Does the Tree grow again? Do you still wear the Locket? Have you known the thalasse?"

"We can't find the Hidden Garden. We may never plant the Tree or have thalasse. May having Piper back again be as the thalasse to you," said Bird.

"If you ever plant the Tree, would you bring me some thalasse?" asked Piper, who listened nearby.

"Me too," said Twist.

Bird promised she would.

RENDARREN'S troops had much damaged Seahold, but home and garden-making were Soladin's great gifts. Aided by many servants, she soon fixed and polished the ancient fastness of the Watchfolk to its former wonder and beyond. She had walls scrubbed from top to bottom, all the silk draperies washed and mended, and hundreds of copper pots scoured to a fare-thee-well. The gardens of Seahold had been overgrown with briers and seedlings from the surrounding forest, but Soladin and her gardeners soon cleared and replanted. Once again the Great Hall of Seahold, with its far wall open to the sea and sky, rang with story and laughter, fiddle and flute. Again the fisherfolk danced their jigs, and the forestfolk performed in their intricate glides.

Farwender continued to languish, for all the care of doctors and Soladin's strengthening tonics. Finally Soladin made a garden just for him, thinking he might rest and heal there. She would not allow the servants to touch this garden but tended it with her own hands. It was a small meadow on a cliff overlooking the sea, enclosed, except at its sea edge, by a wall of stones. Here Soladin grew healing herbs, plumed grasses, wild roses, lavender, and daisies. Soladin never said so, but Bird suspected this sunny retreat looked like the Hidden Garden, now lost forever.

Of all Seahold, Farwender loved this garden best and came often to sit there, on a bench Dren had carved with mermaids and seashells. It was here that Bird found the Watchman, one spring morning of her fifteenth or sixteenth year. He was slumped limply on the bench, gazing out to sea, watching the sea otters sleep on the cliff rocks.

He smiled at Bird and bade her sit with him.

"How are you feeling, papa?" she asked. She called Farwender "papa" every chance she got.

Farwender's eyes were deep in his face, as glinty-dark as a lake at dusk. "I am dying."

"Don't say that. Soladin says you are getting better."

"Soladin refuses to let me speak of it." Farwender sighed. He looked small, withered away. It was hard to imagine he had once been a big man, feared for his strength in battle. "I am worried my death will discourage you. You have been through so much, and who knows what more you must face before the Tree is planted again. Please promise me you will always keep hope in the Seed. For it will be planted—the Tree will grow again."

"I promise," she said. She watched a wave mount and explode on the cliff below. She hoped she could keep her promise.

29

The Tree That Speaks

The Watchfolk blood runs true and stray,
Their hands the Speaking Tree shall slay,
But Slayer's Seed shall Slayer end,
And wake the Tree to life again.

—PROPHECY OF THE HOUSE OF THE WATCHFOLK,
PASSED DOWN BY ORAL TRADITION

A few days later, Farwender lay in bed, too weak to rise. Bird came to the garden alone to pick him field daisies, his favorite flower. Plumetail, one of Finder's kittens, came with her. Finder herself had grown older, and now preferred to spend her days stretched before the kitchen fire, waiting for folk to feed her dainty morsels.

Bird gathered an armload of daisies and then sat on Dren's bench, with its long view of the sea breaking against the cliffs. As Plumetail stalked daffodil shadows, Bird pulled out the Locket. For at least the thousandth time, she studied the etching of the Tree That Speaks. A wave boomed; Bird lifted her eyes to see the cliffs weep with sea wash. The cliffs had curious, stern stone faces that made her think of ancient kings, her grandfathers and great-great-grandfathers.

And then, as a ship long at sea comes to harbor, the words

came to her: "Where the olden stone kings still weep." The rest of the foretelling sang through her mind:

> *Wrapped in light leaves of the life Tree,*
> *Wreathèd by the wings of sparrows,*
> *Beauty's Wen child bares the bright Seed,*
> *Small one come in kindness plants it.*
> *Where the Treekeep tends and deep digs,*
> *Where the sea kind cry from scarp-sky,*
> *Where the olden stone kings still weep,*
> *There the Holder spends his splendor.*

Then she knew. The cliffs were the "olden stone kings." Soladin, the "Treekeep," fiercely tended this ground with her own hands. The otters and gulls were the "sea kind," and "scarp-sky" meant the cliffs and air above them. The "spending of splendor" was both the crashing of the waves against the cliff and the Seed itself, dying in order to grow into the Tree. Everybody had always thought the foretelling described the old Hidden Garden, but instead it described a new place—this one.

A gull cried, a wave smashed, and the stone faces wept again. Bird opened the Locket. The Seed burned as a candle flame, steady despite the gusty wind. It gave no sign that this was the moment to plant it.

From inside the Locket, Bird removed the glass vial, snapped it in two, and shook the Seed into her hand. It winked on her palm. If the Seed hadn't winked, she wouldn't have known for sure it was there. It was that small.

Where should she plant it? Next to the gate? Next to the cliff? In the sunniest corner? She would let the Seed decide. She walked through daisies and bright green grass to the middle of the garden, then closed her eyes and spun. Sometime, somewhere, as she was spinning, she opened her hand, and let the Seed fly into the garden. Then she stopped spinning and looked into her hand. Nothing winked. The Seed was gone. Plumetail didn't notice Bird spinning. The young cat was busy hunting potato bugs.

A dreadful, awesome silence came, and grew and grew. Bird was afraid. It was as when she stood in the surf and felt a wave pull back and back against her, and knew that the longer the wave pulled back, the bigger it would be when it crashed on her head.

She scanned the garden, looking for something to happen. And it did. In a corner not far from a wall and not far from the sea, a sapling popped out of the ground; it actually made a popping noise. Plumetail heard it, and stopped hunting potato bugs to watch. The Tree grew quickly, making creaking, cracking sounds, shooting out limbs here and there. The limbs shook themselves like giant arms, and leaves appeared, great star-shaped leaves bigger than dinner plates. Bird didn't walk closer for a better look for the same reason that she wouldn't have gone near to someone practicing sword-fighting: She didn't want to get accidentally hit.

After a while, the Tree seemed to stop growing. By now it was about the size of a small barn, round and wide, casting a dense shade. Its spring green leaves rustled as if whispering secrets. Bird waited a few moments to be sure the Tree was fin-ished. Then she ran to it. She threw her arms around it and kissed its scratchy bark.

Some of the Tree's branches were low to the ground. Bird thought for a moment of climbing it—it had such a friendly feel—but right then it began shaking again. She jumped back. As doves from a magician's hand, huge violet flowers ap-peared, the shape and size of trumpets. They filled the air with freshness beyond sea winds. The purple flowers rained to the ground, falling all over her and completely, for a moment, burying Plumetail, until the cat pounced free and ran away to another part of the garden. Bird gathered an armful of purple flowers and threw them into the sky.

Now fruits began to form on the Tree's branches. At first they looked like tiny pearls, but they quickly grew. Their pearly color deepened and warmed to gold, and they reached a comfortable size for holding, like an orange or apple.

Then the Tree That Speaks seemed truly complete. It stood demurely in the morning sun, its branches gnarled as if by cen-turies. It appeared to be a kindly old Tree, in which children climbed and made forts.

Bird picked the nearest golden fruit and star-shaped leaf and ran as fast as she could to find Farwender and Soladin.

NEWS spread quickly that the Tree That Speaks lived again, and everyone in Wen clamored for thalasse. As Soladin was Treekeeper, it was her duty to harvest the sap that was the tha-lasse, and this she did, wounding the Tree That Speaks with a silver knife and collecting its glimmering lifeblood in a silver bucket. Both the knife and the bucket were of ancient work and sacred to the folk of Wen.

Soon after, Soladin and Farwender partook of the thalasse together. It was a private matter, and neither of them spoke of it for many years. From that time forward, Farwender's wound was healed, and Soladin ceased to grieve for her misdeeds. She became instead the most joyful of women, although she still wielded her sharp tongue on occasion. Whenever the thalasse was mentioned, Soladin wept.

Bird wished she could take the thalasse with Stoke, but she knew he would never come home until all of his comrades could come with him. So she sent messages to Issie and Dren that the three of them might receive the thalasse together.

Dren arrived at Seahold the next day, taller than Farwender and thinner than Soladin. His tawny hair still poked up in back. "Where's Issie?" were his first words, after greetings.

Issie arrived four days later. Bird was shocked to see that Issie now wore a long gray tunic, the garb of the sisters of the quiet houses. Her golden curls were hidden under a headscarf.

"You took vows?" Bird asked, when they had a moment to themselves.

"Yes."

"Does that mean you will always have to wear those ugly clothes and live in a quiet house and help sick people?"

Issie smiled. "Yes."

"But what about getting married and having babies?"

"I won't be doing that."

"Dren will be disappointed to hear your news," said Bird.

"What's *your* news? Is Soladin driving you crazy with her training lessons?"

"My big news," said Bird, "is that I'm not going to be Watchwoman. Soladin is pregnant. I didn't want to be Watchwoman anyway. All you do is listen to people complain about each other, make long speeches, and sit through other people making long speeches."

"What do you hope for from the thalasse?"

"Guess," said Bird.

"Something about Stoke," said Issie.

"Right. For Stoke to come home and stay home forever. Will this fighting ever be over?"

Issie gave Bird a hug.

NEXT day, a cool spring morning, Bird, Issie, and Dren went with Farwender to the garden. Farwender administered the thalasse to each of his adopted children. He anointed Bird last of all. "Bird, my child, receive the touch of the Holder."

Bird listened and watched. Waves cracked and washed against the cliffs. Issie smiled. Dren looked up into the sky. A hummingbird chased a butterfly.

And then, all at once, Bird felt a goodness wash through her that made every other thing she had ever known, no matter how sweet or clean, seem somehow tainted or shadowed. Then she knew the Holder had kept her all the days of her life. His hands had wrapped her in her star blanket and brought her to Old Hunch. He had guided Farwender to Graynok Market. He had caused Finder to jump into the middle of the feast just in time to save her from Rendarren. He had given her Benwin's scarred hand to hold her first night in Rendarren's cage. He was the whirlwind in her dream and the small square of light in her dungeon cell. He had given her the wit and courage to bring Rendarren to his death, and the understanding of where to plant the Seed. Always the Holder had watched over her, and had held her in His arms as a father holds a child. More than Rendarren, who had begotten her, or even Farwender, who loved her, the Holder was her father. Then Bird knew who she was: She was a Treekeeper. She had been a Treekeeper for a long time, ever since she had accepted the task of carrying the Seed to the garden.

All this came to Bird in a moment. In that moment, she was changed forever, because she knew how much she was loved. A lark that nested in the Tree burst into song and Bird sang with it, a flood of bright clear notes.

The Holder gave Issie the gift of true words so her stories would inspire and enchant. He endowed Dren with skill beyond craft or care, with chisel, knife, and hammer. Everything Dren made afterward held some power of thalasse.

In the days that followed, the Wenfolk came to the quiet houses often and freely, and received the thalasse, and the eyes of their hearts were opened. Soladin was pleased though not surprised to find Bird chosen as Treekeeper, and trained her in her duties. With his new skill, Dren made another Key That Sees, and when he placed it into Bird's hands, the garden of the Tree That Speaks hid itself again, so that only Bird could find it.

Then Bird took the crystal vial Stoke had given her, the

same vial that had carried thalasse to Piper long ago. She filled it with thalasse, sealed it with a silver top of Dren's making, and sent it to Stoke by the fastest, most trustworthy messenger. But she did not see Stoke, or know the Holder's gift to him, for a long time after.

EPILOGUE

It was Farwender's fancy that we would do as in the former days and receive the thalasse at the altar in the woods near Gilladoor, although it was much overgrown with berry brambles. I agreed, for there the Treekeepers of Wen have received thalasse for hundreds of years, but I refused to wear a white cloak or bring daisies as I had done as a maiden. I came in the rags I wore in Rendarren's dungeon, and brought only myself as an offering.

The forest was fragile with dawn light and sea mist. When I arrived, Farwender was already there, so ill he could scarcely stand, lighting altar candles with a trembling hand.

Farwender greeted me as is custom. "Lady Soladin, may the Holder quicken your mind with truth."

And I gave the ancient reply. "Lord Farwender, may the Holder soften your heart with love."

Farwender grinned at me, probably trying to help me feel less afraid. I knelt, and waited. He came to me and put one arm about my waist. I let him touch my forehead with the precious oil that brings glimpses of truth. "Now if you would do likewise," he said, holding out the thalasse cup to me. I anointed his dear creased brow.

And then, as Farwender embraced me, the truth came to me,

and at last I knew that Farwender was right, that the darkness
was past, that the Holder's arms held me as surely as Farwender's, that I was forgiven.

—*CONFESSIONS,* BY SOLADIN LEAFSTAR,

TREEKEEPER OF WEN